KILLINGFORD

Borgo Press Fiction by ROBERT REGINALD

THE NOVA EUROPA FANTASY SAGA

KILLINGFORD

THE HIEROMONK'S TALE, BOOK TWO

BEING THE SECOND ROMANCE OF NOVA EUROPA

ROBERT REGINALD

THE BORGO PRESS

MMXIII

KILLINGFORD

FIRST BORGO PRESS EDITION

Published by Wildside Press LLC

www.wildsidebooks.com

DEDICATION

For the members of the English Department
at Gonzaga University between 1965-1969,
to whom I'll always be grateful for their very
kind advice and consent, especially:

Fran J. Polek
William P. Safranek
Franz K. Schneider
John P. Sisk

(with thanks to Dean Patricia Terry for her help)

—And for Katherine Kurtz,
for giving me permission

CONTENTS

L'ENVOI

But the bravest are surely those who have the clearest vision of what is before them, glory and danger alike, and notwithstanding go out to meet it.

—Thucydides

AUTHOR'S NOTE

For those of you who care about such things, this novel is an alternate history set in a Europe whose geographic features are similar or even identical to our own, with the major (but not sole) divergence from our timeline having occurred in the year 363 AD, when Roman Emperor Julian the Apostate, Constantine I's cousin, was *not* killed in battle against the Persians (as he was in our world), but lived on for another forty years.

For the geographic and personal names herein, I used mostly Slavic, Hungarian, German, and Greek models; there are no silent letters in such constructs. Forward accents are intended to provide guides to stress in Slavic words, such emphasis often appearing in locations unfamiliar to westerners; in Hungarian names, however, the accents merely indicate differences in vowel sounds. I've employed circumflexes in Greek words to distinguish between the letters epsilon and êta, and omicron and ômega. Umlauts can denote gutteral vowel sounds—or dress up otherwise pedestrian names. The letter "ß" stands for "ss."

In the end, of course, I have my own ideas about pronunciation, and each reader will undoubtedly have hers or his. Mangle them as ye will, folks, and no one will be the wiser, unless you actually hear me read a passage someday, and then you can tell me, with as haughty an air as possible, that I've got it all wrong! I do try to have fun when creating these things; some of the names here have been invented from the flimsiest of constructs, bearing no discernible relationship to anything that anyone but I will ever be able to determine. Oh, well!

PROLOGUE

"I ENDLESSLY REPEAT THE STORY OF THOSE DAYS"

Anno Domini 1241
Anno Juliani 881

Always, the marriage!

Her couselors were ever at her heels, nipping away like a pack of curs worrying a fox, and barking and snarling all the while. Gad, if she could just get them to SHUT UP and leave her alone for half a day!

But of course, they never would.

Maybe, she thought, just maybe she should make a virtue of necessity, as the old saying went. Perhaps she should find someone who could easily be controlled, and, uh, wouldn't be capable of siring an heir—at least while she was still technically able of producing one. One of the womanish sirs who huddled so closely 'round the throne, as if to keep warm from the heat that she generated as the center of the state—someone like Count Maltesia or Lord Baniszow. Now, *they* wouldn't be any trouble!

After all, it wasn't as if there were any *lack* of heirs. *Au contraire*: they proliferated in each and every corner of Kórynthia, and even outside the realm—first, second, third, or greater cousins, all wanting to sit high—so high—on that Obsidian Throne. Oh, if only they understood how hard and uncaring that seat really was!

She would pick one of them, in the end. She would have to,

or risk civil war when she was gone.

She walked over to the floor-length metal mirror mounted on the wall of her bedroom. It was an ancient artifact, passed down, so the story went, from old Tighris himself, *primus* of their line of monarchs and mages, whose origins were fogged amidst ungraspable wisps of legend and fable. This great shining speculum, this self-reflecting slab of *albaurum*, was a major seat of power—this much she knew, this much she could ken through her own magely senses. It was no ordinary transit device.

"*What* are you?" she murmured out loud. Her own image, the reversed portrait of Queen Grigorÿna herself, mouthed the words back at her.

Then: "*Who* are you?" said the picture in the mirror, and the unexpected retort caused her to step back.

She slowly and carefully reached out to touch the surface of the white-gold instrument, and almost had the sense, that if she had only known how, she could have roamed the universe itself. But she didn't have the knowledge, and there was no one left to teach her. No one but...but...well, she couldn't go there, didn't dare to go there.

She sighed, long and loud, and finally turned away. She walked over to the open exit to the balcony, stepped outside, and placed her two hands on the stone railing. A bronze gargoyle grinned wickedly back at her from the left-hand wall, and a cuprous dragon's head snarled back a warning from the right. "Keep your distance," it said.

Where was she? What was she doing?

Ah, yes. She breathed in the cool night air, savoring the attar of the aridian blossoms that only unveiled their large pale faces to the dark.

Her history. Her history of the Great War in Nova Europa that had been waged when she was a little girl. The conflict that had destroyed so many of her family and so much of the heritage of two nations.

She'd now completed her chronology of the events leading up to the turning point of the war—of how the Court of Paltyrrha had been seemingly subverted from within, how her grandfather, King Kipriyán III, had been plagued on all sides with the deterioration of the body politic, how a series of attacks and outright murders had pushed the old monarch towards conflict with Pommerelia, and how the strange albino mage known as Melanthrix had somehow been ever at the center of events—and, many believed, the cause of them.

The problem was this: she could find dozens of sources giving accounts of the climactic battle itself—of Killingford—but none that told her what had happened at the very end. They were all...muddled—yes, that was the right word. Even the participants did not understand the events.

Those whom she would question were either dead...or worse. And she dare not step beyond the boundaries imposed upon her by...well, by those who could not be named.

But Killingford had happened in the year 845 of the Era of the Emperor Julian—and that was thirty-six years ago. None of the major commanders who'd participated in the war between Kórynthia and Pommerelia still lived. Only some of the junior officers.

What about one of them? But who?

As a breeze from the Hanging Garden ruffled her dark hair, the Queen thought and thought and thought. Who was left?

And then it hit her: Lord Maurin! The Count of Kosnick! Somewhere she'd read a history of the war by...—who was it, Duodène d'Écosse?—that had cited the Count's memoir of Killingford as one of his primary sources for the great battle. And Maurin, she well knew, was still active, a man of perhaps five-and-sixty years. She would send a note to Kosnicksberg in the morning. Maybe he could tell her what she needed to know.

* * * * * *

Several days later, on the Feast of St. Michael the Archangel, also known as Michaelmas, the Count Maurin III was ushered into her private conference room.

"Leave us!" she ordered Master Svyet, when Maurin had settled on the settee across from her. He was older than she'd remembered, with hair going white and waist going wide—or at least wider than it had been. She hoped his mind hadn't followed suit.

"To what do we owe this honor, Majesty?" he finally asked, sipping slowly at the ruddy wine.

"We wish your assistance with a tome of *historia* we are preparing," she said. "We require your memories of that time three and one-half decades ago when our nation was at war with the Kingdom of Pommerelia. Do you still recall those days?"

The nobleman very deliberately put his drink down on a square wooden table set to one side of his chair. Then he looked up at her, and stared unblinkingly into her eyes; finally, she was the one who had to look away.

"Majesty," he said at last, "there isn't a night that passes that I don't revisit Killingford and all the horrors that I experienced there. I can't escape those memories. There isn't a day that I don't recall all of the men who died on those Pommerelian hills and fields—died senselessly, in my estimation."

"That is not the official position of the state," Grigorÿna said.

"Perhaps," he said. "But it is *my* position, Lady. And I was there—you weren't. With respect."

"Would you tell me about it?" she finally asked.

"How can I not?" he said. "I relate it constantly to myself—to anyone, actually, who wants to hear (or doesn't). I endlessly repeat the story of those days. *How can I not, Majesty?*"

"Then do tell *me*. Please."

And then he began unraveling his tale of the greatest battle that Nova Europa had ever experienced.

CHAPTER ONE
"HE WANTS US TO FEEL FEAR"

Anno Domini 1205
Anno Juliani 845

During the early Spring the preparations for the expedition moved forward rapidly. By mid-April, the first contingents of troops were already gathering at Katonaí Field west of Paltyr-rha, and on the Feast of Saint Zênôn, King Kipriyán decided to conduct a formal review of the soldiers who had assembled there. An official inspection was ordered for the first part of the morning, at *tritê*.

An hour before that time, General Lord Feognóst was in a state of unrestrained panic. Thousands of men were milling about on the muddy plain, trying to find their positions. Horses were still being saddled, draft animals had yet to be harnessed, several heavy supply wagons had tipped over, and all was in chaos.

"Get those men in order," the general shouted at Commander Reményi.

His voice was hoarse.

"And you!" he yelled, turning to the cowering figure of Commander Rónai, "get those bloody beasts back under control."

Slowly but certainly, the impossible was accomplished, and the conscripts began to form in orderly ranks, company by company. The few mounts that absolutely wouldn't cooperate were taken back to the stables, but most were restrained and suitably decked out for parade. Their riders stood stiffly at attention beside their brushed and curried steeds, sweaty and uncomfortable in black leather boots polished to a "fare-thee-well" and bright new dress uniforms that designated, by color and cut, each person's rank and place.

They were as ready as they were going to be when the king and his sons finally appeared, riding out gloriously, streamers flying, from Saint Ignatios's Gate. Kipriyán paused for a moment to look out over the field, his good eye squinting against the sun.

Then he cleared his voice, and loudly intoned: "Very impressive, general. Kudos to you all."

And he saluted them in grand style.

"Huzzah!" came the general cry, as five thousand men responded as one. *"Axios!"* they cried. "He is worthy! Long live King Kipriyán!"

Then the great monarch, resplendent in his finest military armor, neatly dismounted into the sea of mud that stretched before him, and with his boots squelching, slowly made his way through the ranks, commenting to this man and that on his fine appearance. Finally, he came to the head of the file, saluted the general, and offered his congratulations on a job well done.

Lord Feognóst smiled with pride, and bowed in acknowledgment, jauntily returning the king's salute. Then he unsheathed his sword, and carefully placing it hilt-down into the wet ground, abruptly fell on the sharp blade, killing himself almost instantly.

A moment of wretched silence settled over the soldiers of Katonaí Field as the lifeless body of their commander slowly toppled sideways into the mud. Feognóst's final grin was still frozen on his face.

"Nooo!" shouted the king, leaning over the bloody corpse.

Prince Arkády leaped from his mount and pulled his father back from the gruesome scene.

"Nicky," he ordered his brother, "take the king back to Paltyrrha."

Then to the assembled troops, he shouted: "Who's second in command here?"

"I am, sir," a shaken Rónai said.

The officer stepped forward and saluted.

"Dismiss the assembly," the prince commanded, "and sequester the body. I want a death-probe done at once. You're temporarily promoted to general, subject to confirmation by the king."

"Yes, Highness," the soldier said, promptly turning to his junior officers.

An hour later, Arkády received a report from Fra Jánisar Cantárian, the king's physician, stating that the victim's mind had been wiped almost completely clean, that there was only the hint of a compulsion, although one had certainly been in force, and that Jánisar could not tell the prince how the deed was done or who had done it.

"That's not a great deal of help, Ján...," Arkády began, as he finished reading the doctor's statement.

"Well, sir, it wasn't intended to be," Cantárian said, throwing up his hands in resignation. "Although I've certainly tried, I have to admit that this is beyond my abilities. You need very specialized help to scry this kind of magic."

"Can't you even venture a guess?" the prince said.

"Only this," Jánisar said, "that it comes somewhere from the east. Out beyond Byzantion, I'd say. That's speculation, of course, but I think it's a reasonable one. Although nothing about this business seems at all reasonable to me. I also think someone's mixing magical traditions, which you're not supposed to be able to do, but there it is."

"So how do we combat these attacks?" Arkády asked.

The doctor shook his head.

"I wish I knew, Highness. Kill the one responsible, I'd say, although how you find him and how you do the deed are other matters entirely. My only real advice is the obvious one: be careful. Be extraordinarily careful. Your usual defenses won't work here. You're better off to employ cold, hard steel. And I'll offer another guess for you, too: whoever's doing this will keep on killing over and over again until he's stopped. He enjoys it now."

Arkády rubbed his bearded jaw in weariness.

"Who do *you* think he is?" the prince asked.

Jánisar snorted.

"He could be *anybody* at court," the physician said. "He has to have been present often enough to know the people here, to understand their habits and patterns and the routine of court life, and to gain access to them in some intimate way. This is no outsider, I think. This is one of our own, milord."

"God's teeth!" Arkády said. "And here I've been thinking that this monster was some fiend from Hell trying to claw his way into...."

"Well, sir," the physician said, "I very much doubt it. To me everything points to someone with a grudge, somebody who's been holding a grievance inside for a very long time.

"Just look at what's been happening," he continued. "One by one this individual has been attacking different members of the government, none of them key persons in and of themselves, but each building upon the others. He wants us to feel fear. He feeds on that fear. He laps it up like a catamount slurping blood. It's that *feeling*, that sick feeling, of somebody always watching us, that really spooks me, and makes me think that catching this killer and putting an end to his madness will be a very difficult task indeed. On the surface he'll look completely normal, just like anyone else. Underneath, of course, he's monstrous, but you'll never know that. Until he makes a mistake, of course. I just hope there are still some of us left then...."

"What do you mean?" the prince asked.

"I repeat what I said earlier," the physician said. "This one won't stop, not ever, until he's physically or mentally destroyed by one of us. He has a plan that he intends to fulfill, a scheme that none of us understands yet, and until we do, until we put ourselves into his mind and comprehend what motivates him, we won't be able to find him, unless he's a lot less adept than I think he is. To my mind, this is the worse threat the kingdom has ever faced, worse by far than the Nörrlanders or the Walküri or even"—he laughed—"the Dark-Haired Man."

Arkády questioned Jánisar for a bit longer, but there was nothing more to be gained from the conversation, and each man had important tasks yet to be accomplished. As he hurried back to the city, the prince wondered in his own mind where this investigation would eventually lead before the great wheel of fate turned turtle once again, throwing them all into another cycle. Perhaps, he mused, it was best not to worry overmuch about such matters. There was an old saying among the commonfolk that fit the situation well:

"Man proposes, but God disposes."

CHAPTER TWO
"IS THIS NORMAL?"

Hundreds of miles to the east, deep within the rolling hills of Arrhënë, the Archpriest Athanasios was beginning to develop a real hatred of rain. It had poured without relief now for at least three days, ever since he had transited to the count's palace in Aszkán, and he could not imagine a more miserable existence. One of the servants told him they hadn't seen the sun in two weeks.

"Is this normal?" the hieromonk asked, making ordinary conversation.

"We had one spring thirteen or fourteen years ago where it rained, off and on, for two months," came the reply.

No wonder the place was always so green! he thought, regarding his damp, moldy gear with disgust.

Athanasios had been sent by the War Council to check the inventories of foodstuffs and materiel supporting the Arrhéni levies, which were supposed to gather here in another week for the trek to Paltyrrha. From what he had already seen, however, he doubted that they would be ready to march until mid-May.

Only a thousand men had straggled into the capital thus far, and they were a wretched lot: wet, tattered, and poorly armed with old, rusty weaponry. The higher regions of the county were still snowbound, the rivers were overflowing their banks, and the mud was ubiquitous, in one's footwear, clothing, bedrolls, and food. He had seen one man lose his boots that very afternoon to the sucking grip of the grasping goo, which ofttimes had the consistency of sticky clay pudding, and which in some places reached two or three feet deep.

The boy Count Valentín was doing his best, he supposed, but something more was clearly required.

"Count Sándor," he shouted, as he spotted the commander of the regiment hurrying by, "I still need to talk to you about those supplies...."

But he was ignored. Again.

Why had they sent a cleric to deal with these country rubes? He sighed most heavily, and went back into the storehouse. There wasn't enough food here to keep three thousand Arrhénis happy even for the trek to Paltyrrha, much less for an entire campaign. He looked out the door again, and spotted Lord Valentín *Senior*, the ruling count's uncle and the commander's younger brother, who was visiting from Susafön.

"Your Excellency!" he yelled.

The baron, a powerful man in his early thirties, slid to a stop, and saluted the archpriest, water dripping from his hand.

"Father Athy," he said, "how goes the quartermastering trade?"

"Not well, sir," the monk said, "not well at all. I've tried to convey to Count Sándor that this just won't do. There's not enough food here, there's not enough variety of victuals, and what goods we have are rotting from the damp and being devoured by rats."

"Hmmm. And what did he say?" the baron asked.

"I don't *know* what he said," Athy shouted in frustrated anger, "because he won't talk to me. I can't get an appointment to see him, and he doesn't respond otherwise. What am I supposed to do?"

Valentín scratched his bushy sideburns, idly popping a flea between thumb and finger.

"Well, father, it's like this, see. We had a bad winter here, and there aren't any crops in yet. Nobody in these parts has much in the way of food stocks left after all the cold, wet weather, and we can't just strip the peasants of their last supplies. We'd have a revolt on our hands. So, this is basically all we've got or are going to have. However, don't worry about it: the men'll make do. They always have. They're used to getting by on minimal rations."

Suddenly Athanasios heard his name called, and Count Valentín *Junior* came bounding up, cheerful as a new pup.

"Father Athy, how are you?" said the enthusiastic voice.

"Count Val," the archpriest said with real pleasure, "it's good to see you again, sir."

The lad had been his student at the *Scholê* for two years, one of his more promising pupils there.

"How's your new life?" the priest asked.

He gestured at the camp.

"It's great, father," the boy said. "I just wish I could join this expedition with all the rest of you. But the king says I have to stay in Aszkán to guard the eastern frontier, so stay I will, I guess."

He sighed.

"Uncle Sándy and Uncle Tine will get all the fun, and there won't be any Walküri left for me to kill."

Athanasios snorted.

"Oh, I think there'll be plenty of enemies for you to fight, Val. We never seem to run out. But will you be ready to march on time?"

"Uncle Sándor says we'll be a week or two late," the count said, "but 'we'll get there just the same.' He says we'll try to march for Paltyrrha by the first of May, two weeks from now."

Athanasios looked up at the dark skies threatening even more rain, and shuddered.

"I think it's time I returned to the capital," he said. "I should attend the council meeting scheduled for this afternoon, and I have to report to them on the conditions here. Can I carry any messages from you to court?"

The boy scrunched his face into a grimace.

"I was supposed to write to Stepmamá," he said, "and tell her how I'm doing, but I've been so busy these last two months trying to get the troops organized that...."

"I understand. Do you want me to speak to her?" Athanasios asked.

"Oh, *would* you?" Val said, much relieved. "I don't want her to worry about me."

"I'd be happy to, sir."

The priest pulled his hood up over his head, and shivered.

"Now, lead me to a dry place with a *viridaurum* transit mirror, if you please, and let me out of here. I'll never complain about the heat again."

CHAPTER THREE
"EVERY HAND WILL BE
TURNED AGAINST US"

"...And so, sire," Arkády concluded, speaking before the assembled council members, "we see the same hallmarks as before: an inexplicable death, an empty mind, and faint signs of tampering, with no indication of who did this or why, or even how it was done."

"Thank you, Highness," Gorázd Lord Aboéty said. "Are there any questions?"

The king motioned with his hand, and looked suspiciously around the room with his good eye.

"I want to know who's behind this. And I want him stopped. *Now!*"

Arkády just stared at his father.

"Sire," he said, picking his words carefully, "I'm sure we all share your sentiments, but what do you propose we do? We've exhausted our resources."

"I don't want excuses," Kipriyán shouted back, glaring at each one of his ministers in turn. "I don't want to hear excuses from *any* of you. Someone's been tampering with the minds of my men. It's the Dark-Haired Man, I'll warrant. And if *you're* not capable of finding him, maybe I'd better get someone who can. Well, *I* know what to do, even if you don't. All of my ministers and all of my men must be checked regularly again for signs of mental interference."

"What?" several of the council members shouted in unison.

"Who'll do it?" asked another.

"Since we can't trust any of *your* minds," the king said, looking furtively around the room, "Melanthrix can validate each of you."

"That charlatan!" Lord Vydór said. "He's not even Psairothi. I can't agree to this."

"You'll do what you're ordered to do," Kipriyán said.

Vydór slumped in his chair, his skin pale. Finally, he raised his head and looked the king straight in his good eye.

"No, sire, *I shall not.* I will not continue to participate in this charade, which is contrary both to the laws of God and the laws of man. If that doesn't meet with your royal approval, then you can have my resignation from this council, effective immediately."

He rose from his chair, threw his badge of office on the table, and headed toward the door.

"Arrest that man!" Kipriyán thundered.

Two guards surrounded the baron, who shook off their arms. He turned back to the table.

"So," he said, "now it's come to this. Those who render their advice honestly are to be called traitors. My king, I have followed you loyally for these past twenty years, through battles and tempests and even the thickets of political strife. Twice I saved your life on the field, once in the Åvarswood, once in Tretélgia. No one has been more steadfast than I. *No one.* And you've had no truer friend, my lord. But I'll *not* have my mind tampered with by a non-Psairothi."

Arkády rose in his place.

"Sire," he said, seeking a compromise, "surely there must be another way to settle this. Let Fra Jánisar and his trained associates do the checking. They've investigated all of these recent deaths, they're familiar with the hazards, and they'll do an excellent job."

Metropolitan Timotheos hurriedly broke in to second Arkády's proposal.

"A sound idea, sire," he said. "I assure you that the Church would frown on a non-Christian being involved in such a delicate procedure, particularly when it might affect the innermost workings of the government."

As others around the council room began to chime in with their agreements, Kipriyán was forced to back down.

"Very well, I can see the wisdom of having more than one person involved in the scanning," the monarch said, "although Jánisar himself could also be tainted. Therefore, to provide security against *that* possibility, Doctor Melanthrix will be present as an observer. That's my final word on the subject. Lord Gorázd, order it done. Father Athanasios, record my words. Guards," gesturing to the hapless Lord Vydór, "take the prisoner away.

"Now, let us turn to more positive matters," Kipriyán continued in a more normal voice. "I have confirmed Commander Rónai as General of the Army *ad interim*, pending your recommendations on a possible replacement. We should probably appoint a high-ranking nobleman as a titular leader, since Rónai comes from common stock. I'll expect some suggestions before our next meeting. What I need to know now is the general readiness of our forces to meet the May deadline."

Prince Arkády had been preparing for this moment. Once more he rose in his seat, cleared his throat, and began his summation.

"As of today, sire," he said, "we have approximately five thousand infantry and cavalry gathered west of the city, with another two thousand troops and mercenaries in Bolémiagrad, and perhaps a thousand men each at Mylášgorod and Aszkán. I expect these forces to double within the next two weeks. Equipment has been harder to assemble, given the state of the roads; I would guess we're at one-third complement. Another third may arrive by the first of the month, or it may not. I doubt whether we'll be able to reach our overall target of fifteen to twenty thousand soldiers by then."

He wet his lips with a sip of water.

"The core of the army," he said, "about eight thousand men, consists of the battle-hardened remnants of the forces that fought the northerners over the last two decades. These soldiers are both well-trained and -disciplined, and should provide us with very few problems. We have a similar corps of highly experienced line officers. The remainder of the troops, perhaps half, consists of raw recruits who have never fought an engagement, and who only have a barest idea of which end of the sword to grasp. We're in the process of providing some semblance of instruction to these men, but it's minimal at best."

The prince looked up from his notes.

"I have personally examined all of the major units over the last month, and I worked closely with Lord Feognóst in assessing their effectiveness. His recommendation to you today—I know this for a fact—would have been either to postpone the enterprise, for lack of readiness, or to cancel it altogether. I must concur with his evaluation."

There was a gasp from around the table as the councilors realized what the prince was saying.

"No!" the king roared, rising in his seat. *"Never!* I won't hear of it. We haven't come this far just to retreat. Whatever problems we face are nothing to what the Walküri must be experiencing. This is our best chance in a hundred years. I'm determined to go forward with the expedition as quickly as possible, proceeding with our grand exit from Paltyrrha, as planned, on the first day of May."

Arkády lowered his head and looked at the pattern of the growth rings on the oaken table. He traced one of the whorls with his finger tip, as he pondered his next move.

"Father," he said, looking up again, "I beg you to reconsider. The Walküri may indeed be having similar problems in readying their forces; in fact, I'm sure they are, because I've been receiving assessment reports from our scouts and spies in Pommerelia. But there's a difference.

"When the barbarians invaded Kórynthia," he continued, "our nation was rightfully outraged at the burning of Sevyerovínsk and the murder of thousands of innocent merchants and farmers there and in Arrhénë. They responded with an outpouring of men and materiel that was unprecedented in our history, because they realized that the very existence of the land was at stake. We waged war for an entire generation, finally destroying the barbarians at Åvargorod."

The prince sipped again from the cup of water in front of him.

"But this is *our* enterprise, our doing, and we can expect the people of Pommerelia to react in the same way as we did years ago. Every farmer will be our enemy, every merchant a spy, every boy who can lift a pitchfork will dream of becoming a hero. Every hand will be turned against us, and they will nibble at our heels like a pack of mad dogs. And when we turn to kick them back, they'll scamper away just out of our reach. Sire, I have no doubts about the bravery of our men. I have no doubts about the courage of our leadership. But I do doubt the justice of our cause. The signs are not good. The morale of our men has been lowered by the bizarre suicide of their commander. Cancel this expedition, or at least postpone it until we can get our forces together."

The king's face turned a furious red, and he had to gasp for breath several times, before he could finally force himself to speak.

"I never thought to hear my first-born son utter such nonsense," he said. "If any *one* of my sons wishes to remove himself from the succession"—he looked in Arkády's direction—"speak now, so another may be appointed in his place. If any *one* of my officers wishes to run away home before he soils his pretty dress uniform in battle, let him step forward now, and be retired by the scorn of all the brave men assembled at Katonaí. And if there are any *cowards* present in this room, let them remove themselves without penalty, save one thing only, that *I* shall not speak to them ever again upon this earth. The enterprise shall be launched on schedule."

The prince gazed back at his father with great sadness.

"Sire," he said softly, "I have always been loyal to you, and I will follow you unto the ends of the earth, as your ever-faithful hound. Should you doubt this my word, which is spoken with all of the honor of a member of the House of Tighris, then tell me now, and I shall renounce my rights in favor of my eldest son, Prince Arión."

Again, there was a gasp of disbelief from the assembled lords. No one there had ever heard such acrimony between the royals aired so publicly.

The king began to say something, then paused a moment, obviously in confusion.

"Damn the Dark-Haired Man!" he suddenly bellowed, "damn him, damn him, damn him, damn him," pounding the table in counterpoint with his hands till it shook.

The councilors looked back and forth to each other in consternation.

"This meeting is adjourned!" Kipriyán finally said, beating both of his hands upon the hard oak surface, "adjourned, adjourned, adjourned!"

And so it was.

CHAPTER FOUR
"PRAY FOR US ALL"

Later that afternoon the Holy Synod of the Church of Kórynthia met in formal assembly in the annex of Saint Konstantín's Cathedral in Paltyrrha, presided over by the octogenarian Avraäm IV Kôrbinos, Patriarch of Paltyrrha and All Kórynthia.

"In the name of the Father, and of the Son, and of the Holy Spirit," the old man said, bowing his head. "Let us pray."

After some small time spent in contemplation and self-examination, the secretary of the synod, the Protopresbyter Varlaám Njégosh, introduced the matter which had prompted this meeting. Varlaám was a man of about forty years, distinguished by the prominent hawk nose and widow's peak of his ancient noble family, which hailed from Érskeburg east of Arrhénë.

"My lords spiritual," he said, wheezing, "metropolitans and archbishops, Thrice Holy Patriarch"—he bowed unctuously in the direction of their leader—"a matter has been brought before us that requires your most urgent attention. Permission has been sought by the king to bury the late Lord Feognóst, a suicide, in hallowed ground, something that is clearly forbidden under canon law. Because this is a matter of great import, involving one of the leaders of state, the Archbishop of Paltyrrha"—he again nodded in the direction of Avraäm—"has asked for your advice in synod before rendering a reply to King Kyprianos. What say you?"

Ismaêl Metropolitan of Myláßgorod, whose beard reached

down almost to his broad waist, spoke first, being the senior serving member of the group.

"The law is clear on this matter. If Lord Feognóst died by his own hand, then he must not be interred in hallowed soil."

Metropolitan Timotheos lifted his brows in response.

"According to Fra Jánisar," he said, "the man acted under a compulsion. If another forced him to fall upon his sword, this was murder, and the blame falls on the perpetrator, not on Feognóst. I believe we should give him the benefit of the doubt, and honor him for his service to the king. Let him be buried with his family."

Philoxenos Gôritzos, Metropolitan of Bolémiagrad, agreed: "We must always act as Christians, not only in name, but in deed. If there is any doubt regarding the way in which he died, we should let God decide."

However, Zôïlos apo Prousês, Archbishop of Velyaminó, said: "I disagree. A public suicide cannot be excused or amended. Thousands of his soldiers saw him do it. To allow him to be interred in hallowed ground is to tell the world that we will acquiesce to the demands of the state if enough pressure is put upon us. *No!* A thousand times, I say, *no!*"

But he was outvoted by Eudoxios Metropolitan of Susafön, and by the Metropolitans and Archbishops Angelarios, Hierônymos, Nestorios, Iôsêph, and Konôn, while Kyriakos and Mêtrophanês sided with Ismaêl.

Finally, the patriarch spoke in his quavering voice.

"My brothers," he said, "we can add little to this debate, other than to voice our own dismay at what is happening to our belovèd land. This is Satan's work"—they all murmured their agreement—"and we must take every step necessary to purge this evil from our council halls. Therefore, we propose that the king be requested to allow the Protopresbyter Varlaám to exorcise his court and councilors, and also the generals and officers who will soon be leading our soldiers against the papist-loving Walküri. May we hear your voices united in support of this initiative?"

They all agreed, without dissent, and deputized Metropolitan Timotheos to approach the War Council with the suggestion.

"As far as Lord Feognóst is concerned," Avraäm said, "we propose that he be buried conditionally with his relatives, with the language of the service subtly altered to take into account the unique circumstances of his passing. We do not wish to offend the king, nor do we wish to divide the nation at the time of its great enterprise. We have spoken: let it be recorded," he ordered Varlaám.

"Are there any other matters to be brought before this gathering?" he asked.

"Most Holy Patriarch," Timotheos stated, "I again raise the issue of the vacant bishopric of Söpróny in Gärrewestfählen, and propose that the Archpriest Athanasios Hokhanêmsos would be a most suitable candidate to fill that position."

Metropolitan Ismaêl smiled his crooked smile, showing several teeth yellowed and furrowed like the well-worn fangs of some wild beast.

"We have heard this one before, brethren," he said, "and I for one do not wish to hear of it again. The career of this Athanasios has been focused exclusively on the *Megalê Scholê*, and while this is an honorable position, to be sure, which none of us should scorn, nonetheless it has provided insufficient experience for the administration of an episcopal see. *I* propose the Archpriest Samouêl Kontarês, who has managed his several parish assignments with great skill during the last fifteen years."

After much discussion, Ismaêl's candidate was elected, by a vote of seven to five, several of Timotheos's supporters being swayed by the evident competence of Kontarês, who was promptly confirmed in his new office by the patriarch. The consecration of the new bishop was scheduled for a week hence. Then the synod quietly adjourned.

But Timotheos remained behind to discuss matters with his mentor.

"I'm very sorry, Timósha," the older man said, looking every bit his eighty years, "you have not made a friend today."

"Ismaêl was never a friend, holy father," the metropolitan said, "and I'd rather have his enmity displayed openly in the pasture than hidden somewhere in the vale. I didn't really expect to win the appointment for Afanásy. I'm merely laying the foundation for the future."

"My son, my son," the patriarch said, clucking his tongue, "your deviousness will be your undoing one day. These men are not as stupid as you sometimes think, and they resent being manipulated, particularly old Ismaêl, even though *I* know and *he* knows that you thereby accomplish some ultimate great good for the church. But falter just once, Timósha, and they'll turn on you, particularly after I'm gone. How will you come to sit in this chair by acting so foolishly?"

"I don't want to sit in that chair, father," the cleric said.

"What does *that* have to do with anything?" Avraäm said. "Do you think that *I* ever did? Do you think that I craved the power and the glory of leading the church? I refused the honor at first, did you know that? No, I see by your reaction that you didn't.

"Well, twice I turned them down, and I was determined to avoid the burden altogether, if necessary by returning to the cloister. Then Ismaêl, yes, that very one, he came to me privily and said that I must accept for the good of the church, that there was no one else who could assume the reins at that place and at that time without causing a division in the ranks. And so I was persuaded to relent. I think he regrets his advice now, yes I do.

"But that's the way that God works, my dear Timósha. You think that you can oppose what He wants, and then, *poof!*, suddenly things are turned upside down, and you're acting on His behalf, just as our poor metropolitan did. Well, my time here is nearly done."

"No, no, father," the metropolitan said, "you'll be guiding us for years yet to come."

"Don't humor me," the octagenarian said. "I've been patriarch for a great many cycles now, as you well know, and I've been subject throughout that entire period to king and prince and metropolitan, all trying to get the 'old man' to do what *they* want.

"I attempt very hard to see things as they are. I know that I'm dying, at the very time when we are facing the worse crisis to affect our people in a generation, and I also know that you understand this full well, and have already begun calculating the considerations and consequences thereof. But you forget, Timotheos, that however much *you* plan, you can never comprehend or circumvent *God*'s plan for you, or for this Church, or for this land. I know that you mean well, but there's an arrogance yet in you that must be tamed if you're to rule wisely."

"But you just said, father," the prelate said, "that God will dispose of all of our prideful prognostications."

"Don't play the sophist with me, Timósha," Avraäm said, "it doesn't become you. You *will* be patriarch, I can see this in my dreams, oh thank the Lord for them, and they're true dreams, I'm convinced, but the how and the why and the when, I do not know. I'm comforted, however, by this knowledge as I approach the limits of my tenure here, because I know that in the end you'll do the right thing, that you'll follow the pathways that I laid down for you so many years ago, that you'll be a credit both to this office and to the Holy Church."

"I'd still like to find a decent position for Afanásy," Timotheos said.

The patriarch just laughed, long and hard.

"Oh, foolish, foolish man, oh you with so great a mind and so little faith." He chuckled. "Father Athanasios will *also* be patriarch, this too I have seen, and nothing that you or he can do will alter that fact."

"Afanásy?" the younger priest said, astonished by the information.

"Afanásy," the old man said. "You go on playing your games, Father Timotheos, you play them as much as you want, but there is only one game in the sight of the Lord, and you, both of you, will have to decide in due course how *you* will respond to the love that He entrusts unto you, when you have the guidance of the Holy Church as your sole responsibility.

"But do not despair. For as much as He grants you the authority, so too will He give you the strength that you will need to face the perils yet to come. I will not be there, except in spirit, always that, but He is eternal. He will support you. He will guide you. He will not fail you.

"Alas, I am but a frail vessel, and I must now take my rest. I apologize, my old friend, for scaring you in this way, but you have become, at times, rather overcomplacent and overcomfortable with your position, and a man needs to reflect every so often upon the true and vital things of his existence.

"Now let me bless you before I go. May the Body and Blood of Jesus Christ watch over you, comfort you, and give you direction, throughout all of the days of your life. Amen."

"Amen," Timotheos said. "God go with you, father."

"He is always there if you let Him enter your heart, Timósha. Find a way to lead us home to Him, my son. And pray for me. Pray for us all."

CHAPTER FIVE
"WE ARE ALIVE!"

The next two weeks were spent in frenzied activity, as the great expedition to Pommerelia began taking shape outside of Paltyrrha. The rain continued off and on in desultory fashion, occasionally ceasing long enough for the sun to lay a crust on top of the ever-present mud, but the men became used to the bad conditions, and even began joking about them.

By the first day of May, the Feast of Saint Stachys the Stigmatized, eleven thousand soldiers had gathered at Katonaí Field west of the city, with the Arrhéni, Kórynthi, Luristáni, Vorónali, and Velyaminóli contingents still to arrive. Four thousand more troops were already encamped around Myláßgorod, their destination to the west, and another five thousand at Bolémiagrad. Contrary to almost everyone's expectations except the king's, the enterprise was moving forward very rapidly.

The king had picked the first of May as the official leave-taking of the army for many good reasons, primary among them being the fact that this was traditionally the beginning of the warm season in Kórynthia, and the end of the monsoon rains. With the onset of the milder weather, the men could see the evidence around them of things sprouting everywhere, a sure sign of renewal. The optimism generated by all this greenery and the lessening storms had offset the depression following Lord Feognóst's public suicide, an event that still hadn't been adequately explained by the king's physicians, plus the announcement the week before of the passing of the son of

Prince Pankratz. Prince Alexander had perished of the creeping colick at the age of just six months.

But nothing of an unusual nature had occurred in the interim, save a tremor two evenings before that had jolted most everyone from their sound sleep, but had passed so quickly that many could not even identify what it was. Earthquakes were common in Paltyrrha, and anyone over the age of twenty-five remembered all too well the great quake of 1188, which had leveled part of the city.

The leaders of the expedition gathered at the hour of *tritê* at Saint Konstantín's Cathedral in the center of the town, there to receive the official blessing of the Thrice Holy Patriarch Avraäm IV. After the shaky old primate had celebrated mass, given his benediction, sprinkled them with holy water, and distributed the consecrated bread and wine that represented in sacramental form the body and blood of Our Lord Jesus Christ, he and half of his synod prepared to embark with the king's army, for it was only fitting, he was heard to utter, that they suffer the same risks as the others.

"God will protect us," he insisted, "He will watch over us all."

From the Cathedral they marched as one body to Tighrishály Palace, where the Princess Arrhiána and Prince Andruin, the newly named Regents of the Kingdom in Kipriyán's absence, were waiting for them, together with the womenfolk and children of the royal family and the high councilors of state. Many were the tears and the huzzahs that were exchanged that day, and many the promises made of great victories and happy returns. Such are the gentle lies that loved ones tell each other, that they may sleep more soundly at night.

King Kyprianos kissed his son and daughter on each cheek, and gave them their sashes of office. Metropolitan Ismaêl, the ranking member of the Holy Synod, was appointed *Locum Tenens* of the Holy Church by the patriarch.

Prince Ezzö and his eldest grandson, Prince Pankratz, the real commander of the northern army, then made their farewells; later that day they would transit to their camp near Bolémiagrad, where they would lead the northern Kórynthi army into Einwegflasche. King Humfried v kissed his father and eldest son gently, and was actually seen to brush away a tear from his eye as he bid them "*adieu.*" Many at court had begun to comment that the Old Pretender Ezzö was starting to fail in his mind, especially since the unfortunate passing of his son Adolphos the previous winter. Still, he made a formidable presence on this most auspicious occasion, dressed in shiny armor with plumes a-flying, and carefully seated upright in his saddle.

Finally, they were ready to begin at about the hour of *hektê*, which is called *sext* in the west. The king, in heavy battle armor, was helped onto his new stallion, a mighty gray called Szürke, signaling his Elite Guard and chief officers to follow suit. As the command to mount rang out, the dark clouds parted briefly, allowing a slender shaft of sunlight to bathe the monarch in its reflected glow. A brilliant flash of gold ricocheted from the king's crown, blinding the onlookers, and causing awed comments all around. The Guard spontaneously saluted their monarch with their *kiliçs* raised on high. God had officially smiled on the expedition.

They began moving out, but as they started to pass through Saint Konstantín's Square, in front of the great onion-domed cathedral of the same name, suddenly an earthquake rocked the capital once again, rattling windows and nerves alike. While they paused, looking at each other and trying to gauge the strength of the temblor, a second, more severe jolt struck, cracking the statue of King Tamás at the center of the square. The bronze horse on which the dead king was mounted almost seemed to trot free from its moorings, causing the entire structure to slide sideways towards the royal party. King Kipriyán spurred Szürke just in time to avoid being impaled by the outstretched sword of Tamás, who crumbled into pieces when he finally hit the ground. Inside, as they could all see, the statue was rotten clean through with pale green rust.

"Is anyone hurt?" Kipriyán yelled over the din. "Report!"

A few moments later, after consulting with his aides, Prince Arkády spurred his horse into motion, broke free from the chaos, and rode quickly to his father from the other side. He glanced rapidly to his right, then to his left, trying to gauge some estimate of any additional damage they might have suffered.

"Sire," he said, as he wheeled to a stop beside Kipriyán, "several men were cut by flying *débris*, and one horse went lame when he slipped on the rubble. Princess Arrhiána is sending physicians to treat the wounded, as well as workers to begin the clean-up."

The king examined the expectant faces peering up at him, waiting for some direction.

"The Walküri have done their worst," he shouted to the gathered throng, brandishing his sword and waving it over his head, "and they have utterly failed. Look around you. We are alive, we are well, we are strong, we are victorious! Let the *jihad* commence! *Vive la Corynthe!*" he added, using the Gallic dialect which was then the fashion of the nobility at court.

Raucous cheers rattled the eaves of the buildings surrounding the square, even more than the temblor had, and the spirits of the officers and their men, so low a few moments earlier, soared high above the dome of Saint Konstantín's. Certain of victory, assured of God's good will, King Kipriyán and his army marched west out of Paltyrrha, exiting at the Gate of Saint Ignatios, and being joined shortly thereafter by the thousands of soldiers waiting for them at Katonaí Field. Even trampling through the sticky mud, they made a grand sight, ranged row by row in perfect order, their spears reaching up into the sky to prod the very angels themselves into action.

The enterprise was finally launched!

CHAPTER SIX
"DON'T FORGET TO TURN THE OTHER CHEEK!"

Three miles west of the city of Paltyrrha, the Archpriest Athanasios was trying very hard to find a comfortable position for his numb posterior and aching thighs. The raggedy gray donkey called Dyskolos had certainly lived up to his name, being difficult, poky, and not at all inclined to obey a man of the cloth. Without any warning, he would suddenly speed up to a bone-jarring trot, bypassing all the men marching in line, who would encourage the evil beast with catcalls, insults, and laughter, and occasionally with jabs of their sharp spears. Then the beast would jerk to a complete stop, allowing the jeering foot soldiers to catch up and pass them again, while Athanasios, legs pumping and arms waving, angrily tried to spur the tyrant forward.

It had been a frustrating afternoon for the priest, inexperienced rider that he was, but he attempted to pass the time as profitably as he could by saying his daily prayers, and beseeching God's benign intervention with their dangerous mission. But time and again he found himself distracted by having to attend to the reins, as he held on to his precarious seat.

On his fifth or sixth such run, Dyskolos tried a new maneuver, and succeeded in abruptly bucking Athanasios off over his head, straight into a large mud puddle. The startled priest found himself flat on his back and soaked through, struggling to regain his wind as he stared up at the vacuous face of his obstinate mount. Dyskolos smiled back with bared yellow teeth, having finally rid himself of his unwelcome burden. Then, floppy ears laid back, he stretched out his scrawny neck and shook his head, flinging foam into the priest's face and jingling his bridle jauntily, and braying raucously a few times in unconcealed triumph.

Several soldiers of the Kosnicki Brigade, who were marching right next to them, almost fell over, they were laughing so hard.

"Now, father," one of them yelled, "don't forget to turn the other cheek!"

There were more hoots and guffaws.

"An ass in time saves nine!" another quipped.

The troops behind them began to bunch up as they watched the welcome spectacle of a cleric finally receiving his comeuppance.

Athanasios climbed shakily to his feet, then gazed down at his ruined cloak, his cheeks burning with the shame. He hated being humiliated like this. From the time he was a child, he had disliked being made the brunt of public ridicule or scorn.

"Hey, what's going on here!" shouted the captain of the squad, riding over from the other side of the column.

He was a tall, amiable-looking man in his late thirties, clean-shaven save for a trim mustache, and neatly decked out with light chain mail, helmet and jaunty feather, and military cloak. His gear was beautifully polished, and he sat confidently astride a handsome bay, its shiny black mane and tail floating in the breeze. He gracefully dismounted, and gave the priest a hand, steadying him a bit as Athanasios tried to regain his composure.

"Sorry, father," the officer said, "these rubes don't know any better."

He glared at the assembled soldiers, and vigorously waved them on.

"Don't you have anything better to do?" he yelled. "You! Get along over there. Come on, move it out!"

His men gradually sorted themselves into loose ranks again, and the column started forward.

The captain quickly grabbed Dyskolos's reins to prevent him

from running off, and handed them over to Athanasios, simultaneously inclining his head.

"Sir Maurin von Markstadt, Lord Ézion, at your service, father. You seem to be having a little trouble with your mount."

The hieromonk looked upon his savior with immense gratitude.

"Oh, thank you so much, milord," he said. "I'm the Archpriest Athanasios Hokhanêmsos."

He shook his head in dismay, brushing futilely at his damp clothing.

"I must confess, I don't really know what I'm doing wrong. They showed me how to control the beast, but Dyskolos is the devil himself."

"*Dyskolos*, eh?" The officer snorted. "Oh, I've heard about that one. I think someone was trying to play a joke on you, father. This donkey's a *real* ass."

He cleared his throat as he swallowed a laugh.

"However," the officer said, "we have our ways."

Maurin led Athanasios and his mount off the crowded road and over to a nearby tree. He chose a small, supple limb, broke it off with his bare hands, then carefully stripped it with his knife. He whipped it experimentally through the air a couple of times.

"Yes, that'll do nicely," he muttered to himself.

Then he turned to the priest.

"Would you happen to have an old spare rag," he said, "something you won't be needing again?"

Athanasios pondered a moment. "Well, I think so, milord, but...."

"If you'll get it, please," the captain said, "I'll demonstrate."

The priest rummaged around in his kit, and finally tore a strip from a frayed, well-worn tunic.

"Will this do?" he asked.

"Perfectly," Maurin said, smiling. "You just have to be a little smarter than the beasties," he said, abruptly stepping on the donkey's reins to hold its head momentarily still, and then wrapping the cloth several times around its eyes.

He stepped back to admire his handiwork, tucking in the ragged edge of cloth.

"There, that should fix him. Now you can mount," Maurin instructed the priest.

Athanasios climbed back into the saddle. Dyskolos stirred uncomfortably, badly wanting to be rid of his burden, but uncertain of himself in his blindness.

"You see, father," the officer said, "without his sight, old Dysk here has lost his manhood, so to speak, although he had already lost *that* some years ago, ha ha ha, and so he won't go running off to where he shouldn't be going."

"Well, then, how do I get him to move?" the priest asked.

Maurin handed him the switch.

"Try this, father," he said. "A little application to the appropriate hindparts will work wonders, you'll find."

Sure enough, the beast was quite docile now, and moved when and where the hieromonk directed.

"It's a miracle!" Athanasios said, "a gift from God."

"Not really," Maurin responded. "You just have to outthink them. You'll find that after a few days, friend Dyskolos will have decided that you're the master here, and then you won't need the blind any longer."

"May I ride with you a while, milord?" Athanasios asked.

"Certainly, father, I'd enjoy your company." The captain nodded cheerfully. "But please call me Maury. Most of my friends do."

"And I'm Athy," the priest said, happy to be back in control. "Whence do you hail?"

"From up north," the captain said, "a county called Kosnick. My cousin Dónan's the ruler there."

"Why, I know the place!" Athanasios said. "It's tucked between the crook of the upper Paltyrrh and the Kultúra Rivers, west of Tavársky. Very nice location. But I'd have thought that you would have marched straight south to Myláßgorod. It's much shorter, isn't it?"

"Well, as the crow flies, sure," Maury said. "But the roads are just a mess these days, clogged with wagons and foot-deep mud, and Count Dónan thought we would do better by taking the barges down the Paltyrrh. We had an awful lot of rain up there this spring. It only took us a few weeks to get downstream."

"I see."

The priest's clothes were beginning to dry, and even though he was sure to be sore from his fall, Afanásy was finally feeling more comfortable with his situation. A thought came to mind.

"You look as if you've seen quite a bit of military service," the cleric said.

"'Bout twenty years, off and on," the officer said, "in six-month or one-year stints. I've experienced a lot of action, from the barbarians to bandits to brigands."

Athanasios nodded.

"I rather thought so," he said. "I wonder if you could satisfy my curiosity. Part of my work involves copying documents for the king and his court. The other day I came across a military record that I couldn't decipher. Now, you understand that I'm supposed to know these things, even when I don't. It's a little like handling this donkey: no one wants to hear excuses about why I can't ride, even though I've had very minimal experience in recent years. So I couldn't ask anyone there at court without looking the fool, and I put the pages aside. But a man of your great military experience just might be able to help me."

"Anything I can do, Father Athy," Maurin said.

"Why, thank you, Lord Maury." The archpriest smiled. "Here's my problem. I have an old service record that consists only of a name followed by a series of initials." (He was referring to a document that he'd located earlier that year in the Official State Archives while investigating the mystery enveloping his own past history.)

The captain removed his hat and scratched his head. The sun was bright in the sky and beginning to heat the ground.

"Well, I *have* seen a few of these registers. Usually, they indicate an officer's rank and assignment, in that order, followed by subsequent postings, if he's been transferred to another unit."

"Ah, so the letters 'SL' would be Sublieutenant?" Athanasios asked.

He had already worked that one out for himself.

"Of course," Maury said, "and 'FL' is full Lieutenant, 'CP' Captain, 'CM' Commander, and so on."

"Then what would 'KG' stand for?" the priest asked.

The soldier laughed. "That one's easy," he said, "King's Guards! *Very* elite bunch, reconstituted during the wars with the northerners."

"Of course," Athy said, chuckling along with him, "and what about 'DD'?"

"Hmm." Maurin looked puzzled. "Hmm!" he rumbled again. "Well, I honestly can't think of any unit having those initials. Now you've really got me interested. Just a moment," he continued, "let me, uh, check with someone else who's been around longer than I have. Back in a snap."

The captain pounded further up the column, stopping to talk with an older officer leading another unit. They conversed together for a bit, and then Maurin came trotting back, smiling broadly.

"You almost had me fooled there, Athy," he said, coming alongside the donkey. "I was right. There isn't any troop with that designation. It means 'Detached Duty.' Very rare.

"Usually," he continued, "they're scouts or spies working directly for the king or one of the high councilors of state. They're sometimes given passes that allow them to sequester anybody for questioning whom they wish, or to secure any goods they might need to complete their mission. Basically, they carry the authority of the king on their person.

"I've only knowingly met one or two in my entire career. They're very quiet fellows, operating strictly behind the scenes. They wear no badges and have no units, and you won't even know they exist most of the time, unless they're forced to reveal themselves, and they really don't like doing that. Trained killers, too, very nasty in a fight. Wouldn't mind having a few of them with us for this 'go,' if you know what I mean."

"Indeed I do," Athanasios said absently, reeling from the impact of the information Maurin had given him. Because, if Arik Rufímovich, he who had later become Metropolitan Timotheos, had been on detached duty from the military during the period when he had delivered the child Athanasios to Saint Svyatosláv's Monastery in May of 1166, just *who* was he working for then? *When* exactly had he joined the church? The answers to these questions, if he could find them, probably would tell him all that he needed to know about his origins.

He gradually shifted the conversation to other matters as they moved through the hazy afternoon light west of Paltyrrha. Around them the flies buzzed idly 'round and 'round, cruising in large circles about the horses and their riders and the marching infantry, knowing that they would feast that evening on horse and human dung and other assorted garbage. Life for them was very good indeed.

CHAPTER SEVEN
"A MIGHTY CROP OF BASTARDS"

The column traveled about ten miles that first day, not halting until the pale orange sun was starting to set in the darkening sky.

They erected the king's tent first, both for its symbolism as the monarch's point of command, and even more importantly, because it contained their only reliable transit mirror. Establishing and maintaining a mobile *viridaurum* was notoriously difficult, even for an experienced group of Psairothi, but it was crucial to their operation to be able to communicate regularly with the capital and with the different troops now converging on Myláßgorod.

Prince Arkády was everywhere at once, frantically trying to keep the units together, and pausing for a word here and there with his officers. The experienced ones knew exactly what to do, but the rest had to be taught, step by painfully slow step. Even though they were still deep within their own kingdom, the lords had decided at the last meeting of the War Council to pretend from the very beginning that they were operating in hostile territory, as a training exercise.

Arkády kept an admiring eye on his father, as the king expertly organized the layout of the camp, based on the availability of water and the natural defenses of the place. King Kipriyán had settled down somewhat during the last few weeks, since the shock of Feognóst's suicide. Thankfully, there had been no further incidents, although the prince was under no illusion on that score: more would follow, of that he was certain. They had all been watching each other constantly, looking for the tell-tale signs of hidden workings. Tension was high.

Soon the camp was established, with large, well-stocked tents for the officers, councilors, and major churchmen, and campfires and bedrolls for everyone else. Savory stews were already simmering over the open flames; he could smell the juicy meat and vegetables flavored with field onions and other fresh herbs, so generously if sometimes reluctantly donated by the local farmers. His mouth watered. To his complete surprise, he found himself suddenly ravenous, and hastened off to his own tent, where he had been housed with several of the chief officers of the court.

After everyone had filled their bellies, the king, his sons, and the major lords and councilors gathered around a large bonfire near the monarch's tent. Arkády spied Melanthrix lurking to one side, and his dinner briefly crawled back up his esophagus. Choking down the bile, he lowered his head, and carefully watched the thin figure of the astrologer from the corner of his eye. He had been avoiding contact with the king's boon companion ever since Melanthrix had saved the life of little Ari, the prince's eldest son and heir, but Arkády knew that a time would come soon when he would have need of the philosopher again, and he dreaded that rendezvous-to-come.

The king was in fine form this night, telling stories of the old wars that he had waged, of the great triumphs and narrow escapes that he had known. Everyone loved to hear the tale of the Åvarswood, of how sixteen men had clawed their way through hordes of Northmen and an entire forest finally to rejoin their comrades. There were cheers all around when Kipriyán recounted their joyous reunion with the main army, and how they had pursued and punished the barbarians for weeks, until they were all butchered or enslaved, each and every one.

"Tell us about the great war with Pommerelia," someone suggested.

"But I wasn't there," Kipriyán said, laughing. "Oh, would

that I *had* been. Is there anyone amongst us who has stories to sing about that conflict?"

Athanasios, who was sitting in the background with the other churchmen, was surprised when Metropolitan Timotheos said nothing. He almost spoke up on his mentor's behalf, when he suddenly realized how he would have felt if placed in a similar position.

"Come, come now," the king said, "surely somebody has something to contribute. What about you, friend Melanthrix?"

"Like you, my king, Melanthrix never served," the philosopher said. "But he heard tales, oh yes he did, of what happened in those far-gone days, and of the great King Makáry thy father, and of thy valiant brothers, the Princes Néstor and Karlomán."

"Show us!" came the eager refrain from all sides.

Melanthrix reached into a hidden pocket of his robe, and pulled forth some powder which he sprinkled over the fire, creating a flash that momentarily blinded them, and much putrid green smoke. When they could see again, there was the rotating visage of Makáry I King of Kórynthia, as if he had been there in real life.

Suddenly, the picture dissolved into the image of a column of soldiers, very similar to their own, marching off to war. That faded off into another portrait, and then another, like a series of vivid tapestries, leading them further into the history of the conflict. First came the great victory at Argöliß and the death of King Michael—cheers all around—the early onset of the freezing winter weather that stopped their advance cold, the privations faced by both sides, the second expedition of the following year, the troops assembled before Dürkheim, the siege of that mighty walled city, the trickery of the Walküri and the death of King Makáry—groans from everyone—the retreat to Einwegflasche, the third-year stand of King Ezzö the Elder at Borgösha and the siege of that city, and Ezzö's final suicide that marked the end of the campaign.

No one ventured a word for several moments after the last picture frayed into nonexistence.

"Well," said the king, breaking the silence, "at least I hear that our boys plowed a mighty crop of bastards that year in fresh Pommerelian soil."

Most of the soldiers laughed, but a few men—Arkády, Athanasios, Timotheos, and some others—privately grimaced or said nothing at all. *This* was not an achievement worthy of boasting. Arkády wondered what the poor women had done with their unwanted children; he'd heard tales of dozens being left in the woods by their anguished mothers for the elements and wild animals to eliminate.

The party gradually dissolved into separate knots of men discussing strategy or the practical matters of getting the units moving on the morrow. The king soon rose to retire, ordering all but the pickets off to bed.

CHAPTER EIGHT
"YOU WILL OBEY ONLY ME"

But there was one who roamed far into the hollow of the night that evening, bypassing the guards quite readily, sloughing off his human form for another semblance that was far more comfortable. At the hour of the wolf he silently stood beside Kipriyán's bedroll, and gazed down upon the snoring image of the king, watching the tendrils of beard waver in the exhaled breath of the great ruler. Then he reached down and touched the sleeping beauty on the middle of his forehead, and a green glow swept slowly down over the recumbent body of the monarch, sparing not even his toes.

Suddenly he heard someone coming, and turning halfway towards the entrance, quickly twisted his hands together—*and was gone!*

"Father," said Prince Arkády, opening the tent flap and peering in. "Oh, I'm sorry, I didn't realize you were already asleep."

The king didn't wake, however, and his son was about to take his leave when abruptly he stopped. He sensed a strange fragrance in the air. He took a deep breath, trying to place it in the context of his memory, but the odor eluded him, and gradually diminished even as he tried to draw it closer. He had encountered the taint somewhere before, of that he was certain. Finally, though, he dropped the cloth back over the exit, and headed towards the perimeter to check the pickets.

In the tent, a black moth came to rest on the center of

Kipriyán's chest, its wings lying flat to either side. Another soon joined its sister, and then another and another, until the king's entire body, save only his nose, was enshrouded in a dark, slightly moving cloak.

In his own mind, the king was dreaming of Paltyrrha in the summer of 1164. He was studying the Romanish tongue with Fra Callanus, when the door of the study banged open, and he was abruptly dragged from his tutor by a pair of burly guards whom he had never before seen, and locked away in a window-less storeroom. Once each day these same men brought him bread and cheese and water, and changed his bucket, but they would not respond to his questions, and he was left, finally, with nothing but tears of frustration and anger and fear.

On the tenth day he was half-dragged to a *viridaurum* and taken to Saint Ióv's Church, where his great-uncle, Metropolitan Víktor, was waiting for him by the main altar.

The cleric was imposing in his red cassock and ornate vermilion hat, towering at least two feet over the boy. With his bushy gray beard, he looked like God Himself.

"You may go," the churchman ordered the guards, who immediately departed.

Then he turned to his nephew.

"Your father's dead," he stated, "your brothers too."

"Wh-what?" Kipriyán said, unable to assimilate the message.

He felt as if the underpinnings of his entire world had just been destroyed.

"The king's been killed," Víktor repeated. "I've been named Prince-Regent of Kórynthia by the Royal Council. We have to make a few decisions, Kyprianos."

"What?" the boy stated again.

"Look at me, lad!" the prelate ordered.

He gazed up into that austere face. His great-uncle's eyes were as cold as emerald crystals.

"The king is dead," the regent emphasized once more. "Your brothers are dead. That leaves you the apparent 'heir apparent,' Kyp. But these things aren't so obvious sometimes, are they?"

"I don't understand, sir," Kipriyán responded.

"No, of course you don't," the older man indicated. "Some of us feel that you're not quite kingly material, but I happen to believe that you'll do just fine. What do you think, my boy?"

"I, I,..."

"That's what I thought," the cleric said. "Now, listen to me carefully, Kyprianos. This afternoon you'll be presented to the Royal Council, where you'll be proclaimed King of Kórynthia. I and your grandmother will be your co-regents, but you will obey only me, do you understand? You will follow my every lead, you will respond exactly as I dictate. If you fail to do this, if you fail *me*, boy, he'll come for you in the night."

"Wh-who, sir?" Kipriyán said.

"The Dark-Haired Man!" the metropolitan roared, suddenly transforming himself into the image of a hairy, black beast rising up to the ceiling of the church, ready to devour the lad.

The king screamed out loud, screamed his terror and fear and horror, and he was still shrieking when he awoke in his tent, surrounded by hundreds of fluttering moths that kissed him everywhere he turned. But try as he might, he could not get away.

CHAPTER NINE
"THE ENTERPRISE
WILL PROCEED"

Two weeks later, early on the morning of the Feast of Saint Matthias, the royals, accompanied by the first units of the Kórynthi army, finally reached the gated citadel of Myláßgorod. Behind them snaked a column six miles long, although some of the supply trains were straggling as much as three days behind the main force. The weather had cleared for five straight days out of Paltyrrha, allowing them to make very good time initially; but the rains had started up again on the sixth day, and the cumulative effect of thirty thousand human feet pounding into the same small patch of ground, not to mention several thousand horses and the wheels of a thousand wagons, had churned the roads into runny brown ribbons of slippery mush.

The ancient walled city of Myláßgorod was located on the eastern bank of the Myláß River in the foothills of the Carpates Spinæ, a long, narrow mountain range that angled northwest towards the Baltískoye Mórye, and acted as the border between Kórynthia and Pommerelia. The city was the chief seat of Count Otakar von Tighris-Myláßgorod, who was waiting nervously just inside Saint László's Gate to greet his distant cousin and liege, the king of Kórynthia. The rains had mercifully abated during the last day, and the sun was glittering brightly off his armor as Count Otakar stepped forward, gloved hand raised in welcome.

"All hail, King Kyprianos!" boomed Otakar, sweating

profusely. "Welcome to Myláßgorod, gateway to the Inland Empire."

The king swept his heavily mailed arm around, including his officers and soldiers in the gesture.

"We are most pleased to arrive here, *Cousin*," he intoned, "and we look forward to several days of rest before proceeding through the pass into Pommerelia."

He publicly embraced the count, their mail shirts clanging against one other. There were huzzahs of approval from the assembled brigades.

Otakar motioned for silence.

"Milord," he said, "I invite you and your family and officers to join me for a banquet of celebration this evening. We have also prepared quarters in the city for the higher ranking members of your staff, and hope you will take advantage of this respite to shake loose some of the dust of travel."

And with that they adjourned to the privacy of the citadel within the town.

An hour later the War Council assembled in the count's meeting room to receive an updated assessment of their progress. As had become customary, it was Hereditary Prince Arkády who gave the initial presentation.

"My king, my lords, my generals," he said, brushing the hair back from his forehead. "Twenty-two thousand men are now encamped around Myláßgorod, or soon will be. Six thousand more have gathered in Bolémia, and will be supplemented shortly by another thousand mercenaries. Another four or five thousand soldiers are still in transit here, and may or may not reach us in time to be useful.

"Our main problems seem to be lack of supplies and sanitary facilities. Our chief quartermaster, Navkráty Blagoslávovich, and the King's physician, Fra Jánisar Cantárian, are both available to give you additional details, should you need them. However, I can provide the following summation."

He cleared his throat before continuing. "Many of our supply wagons have been delayed by the awful weather conditions, and at least some of the food they carry has been spoiled by the damp. The first spring crops are only barely starting to come in, and the Myláßi and Susaföni warehouses are almost empty. We're attempting to bring additional supplies upriver on barges from Südmark and Faülniß, but as you know, the Myláß River is only navigable for a short distance after it splits from the Drúna. We've even had to move some crucial foodstuffs through the few transit mirrors, which are already heavily clogged with official travelers.

"Now, as to our second problem," Arkády said, "we lack sufficient sanitation pits to accommodate this many men, and digging additional latrines is almost impossible in these muddy conditions. Already, we are seeing cases of both the typhous and the typhoidous grippe, as well as many other infectious diseases. Fra Jánisar tells me that these will worsen unless we can relocate quickly. More disturbing to me are the ever-increasing reports of foot rot, which the wet weather seems to be fostering. I don't have to tell you, milords, that an army mostly marches on its feet, and if those feet are hurting, our pace will be significantly reduced."

The prince took his seat, inclining his head towards his father's chief minister, the grand vizier.

"Thank you, highness," Lord Gorázd said. "Are there any questions? Yes, Prince Nikolaí."

"I was wondering," the burly warrior said, "if we have any current reports on the situation in the Skopélosz Pass. Just what are we facing at Borgösha?"

Sir Léka d'Örs, the king's Chief Scout, fielded the query.

"The pass is clear of snow and lightly guarded," he said. "Only a thousand Pommerelian soldiers, possibly less, hold Borgösha, under the overall command of Gajus Count Thulden. He's been unable to get supplies from Körvö, due to the Spargö River being over its banks, and very little has trickled down from the north. I hear that Iselin Graf von Einwegflasche is holding on to everything he's got, waiting for Prince Ezzö and Prince Pankratz to dare the Kultúra Pass up north."

"I see." Nikolaí stroked his beard. "And is Prince Pankratz ready to move?"

"*I* can answer that," King Humfried said. "My father and my son have already positioned their forces at Körösladány on the east end of the Kultúra Pass. They're just waiting for the word from Mylåßgorod to proceed. They're ready, all right!"

"Then the enterprise will proceed on schedule," King Kipriyán boomed. "Arkásha, where in the bloody halls of Hadês are those damn'd Arrhénis?"

CHAPTER TEN
"THEY STILL RIDE COWS THERE"

Where, indeed?

That same morning 3,500 soldiers from Arrhénë were just in the process of being ferried across the Paltyrrh River, which was now running dangerously high from the spring runoff.

Princess Arrhiána was watching the proceedings from the *Quai de Saint-Basile*. She was clothed in a rough leather riding habit and cloak, topped by a bright red felt cap with a jaunty pheasant feather plume. Suddenly one barge capsized, drowning twenty or thirty men in the process.

She shook her head. *Those poor soldiers. What will I tell their widows?*, she thought to herself.

"Sándor!" she called out as loudly as she could.

The commander of the Arrhéni Brigade immediately broke free of the group he was instructing, and came trotting over.

Aleksándr Count of Yevpatóriya, or "Sándor," as everyone called him, was about thirty-five years of age, with a florid complexion, broad shoulders, and heavily-muscled arms. His shaggy, auburn hair hung down the back of his neck in knotted strings, although he knew he would have to trim it before going into battle. At present he was totally concerned with the formidable task of getting his brigade across the river. He understood only too well how late they were, and it was a matter of pride to him that his forces make a good showing in the upcoming battle.

"Milady," he said, saluting his sister-in-law politely in front of her guardsmen.

She grabbed his arm and pulled him to one side.

"Sandy," she said, gesturing at the swiftly-running water below the crossing, "I want you to string some additional cables to stabilize the ferries. We just can't continue taking these kinds of losses. We're having problems with almost every trip."

"Yes, princess," he said. "I was about to order the same thing myself. I'll see to it immediately."

Making a small bow in her direction, he ran off downstream to carry out her instructions.

While the new ropes were being lashed to either side of the river bank, Arrhiána heard a contingent of riders galloping rapidly down the *Avenue du Saint-Constantine* behind her. She turned just in time to greet Prince Nikolaí, who dismounted with a flourish, and handed her an official dispatch from the king.

"Nicky!" she squealed with delight, her feather bobbing, "what a pleasant surprise. How are father and our brothers? What news?"

"Sister," the burly prince responded, practically lifting her off her feet with his giant bear hug, and pecking her rather sloppily on both cheeks. He glanced around to make sure that none of his men were watching this unseemly display of affection.

"Can't stay long," he said. "Kásha has ordered me to check on the progress of the Arrhénis, and to report back to him later today."

She turned away from him and pointed at the river.

"Well," she said, grimacing, "there they are in all their glory, and unless we can get more barges *and* ropes *and* experienced men to run them, there they'll stay for another couple of days. Even using bonfires to light up the night, we can't get more than a thousand men across in one day. And that's not even counting their horses and equipment, such as they are."

"God's breath!" he said. "Father's not going to be happy about this. All he ever wants to know is, 'Where are those blasted Arrhénis?'"

"Well, why don't *you* discuss the problem with Sandy yourself."

She nodded her head at the commander conferring with his men a little further down the jetty. Calling an aide, she ordered that he fetch Count Sándor posthaste.

Breathing heavily, the nobleman joined the prince and princess a few moments later.

"Nicky! Great to see you, cousin!" he said, wrapping the prince in a bear hug of his own, and clapping him on the shoulder soundly. "How goes it in Myláßgorod?"

Before answering, Nikolaí suggested they take their discussion to a nearby quay-side tavern, where they settled out front at a rough outdoor table and bench protected from the elements, where they could still keep an eye on the river crossings.

A pretty young serving wench rushed out, wiping her hands on a bright homespun apron. Nikolaí and Sándor called for ale, while Arrhiána opted for hot mulled cider. They were quickly served with drinks and crusty bread, sharp cheese, garlicky sausages, and tiny pickled onions, which the proprietor was only too happy to provide gratis.

The prince settled back to give them both a brief summary of the army's slow trek cross-country, and an account of the difficult conditions in Myláßgorod. He soon had them both laughing uproariously with his tale of the wretched hieromonk and his donkey.

"No!" said Arrhiána, laughing and wiping the tears from her eyes. "The poor man! Why on earth did they put him on such a beast in the first place?"

"Maury thinks it was a joke someone was playing on him," Nikolaí said. "No one knows who assigned that particular animal to Father Athanasios. To give the man credit, he stuck with it and finally mastered the ass, with Maury's help, of course."

The prince took a final swig of ale, wiping his mouth with the back of his hand, then added pointedly:

"All joking aside, father keeps asking what's holding you up, Sandy. That's why he sent me here."

The count threw up his hands in frustration.

"Everything and nothing," he said. "If you can believe it, the roads are even worse in Arrhéně than they are out west. The provisions have been terrible. You can see the difficulties we're having just getting across the Paltyrrh. We're coming as fast as we can, Nick, but it's going to be at least two weeks before we reach Myláßgorod, maybe longer. I can't keep pushing the men this way without giving them a few days' rest at Katonaí Field. As it is, we'll have to reprovision and regroup here, and I don't even expect us to start from the city for another four days. I hear the Voróna and Velyaminóli Brigades are having similar problems; they're still stuck somewhere southeast of us in the hills on the other side of the river."

Nikolaí shook his head. "I don't know what I'm going to tell father, or how he'll react. He's been very difficult of late. One moment he's ready to charge off to war, full of energy and ideas, and the next he's hiding away in his tent, speaking to no one except that thrice-damn'd charlatan, Melanthrix, and blaming everything on 'the Dark-Haired Man.' People are beginning to talk, Rhie. Kásha's doing all he can to maintain control, to give the war effort some kind of direction, but even *he's* had a few clashes with Papá. I'm really beginning to worry about the king's state of mind."

"I know, Nicky," Arrhiána said. "Kásha and I are concerned, too. That 'doctor,' as he calls himself, has completely taken over father's life with his tales of ghosts and goblins. I just can't believe that Papá would place such credence in...."

A yell and a splash quickly turned their attention back to the river, where another barge had tipped under a swell of the rapid current, dumping several men and horses into the fast-flowing water.

"Sorry, cousins, got to run," shouted Sándor, pelting off at full speed toward the ferry post.

Several of his men were heading downstream to rescue the soldiers. Nikolaí and Arrhiána watched one half-drowned man being pulled onto the bank, while the body of another sank out of sight.

Nikolaí sighed and rose from the table, placing several bronze chalkoi in the hands of their protesting host.

"Nice fellow," he said, gesturing toward Sándor. "Is he married?"

"*Nicky! Stop it!*" Arrhiána said. "I've already been wed to one of those boys, and I don't have any desire to marry another. Besides, he's more like a brother to me than anything else."

"Ah," Nikolaí said. "That's why he kept looking at that pretty little cap of yours."

Arrhiána took a half-hearted swipe at her brother, but he ducked in time.

"I suppose you have to leave, too," Arrhiána said, her voice sad.

"As much as I hate to go, big sister," her brother said, "I have my duty." He managed a tight smile. "When all else fails, I still have the Tighris honor to uphold."

"Just don't get yourself killed trying to satisfy that honor, Nicky," Arrhiána said, and then hugged him to her tightly. "I do miss you."

"And I you," he said. "But now I have to go and find you a spouse in Pommerelia, since you obviously don't have enough things to do here, and certainly need the firm guidance of a *very stern husband*. Let's see, now," he said, "I could probably capture that limp-wristed cleric, Prince Magnus Walküre, or maybe his younger brother, what's his name, Prince Jerkin? He's probably not even potty-trained yet."

"Oh, cut it out," his sister said. "I get enough teasing from Kásha. When I marry again, *if* I marry again, you'll be the *last* one I tell. And you should talk: you're betrothed to that empty-headed sprite from Mährenia. Oh, I grant you, she's a pretty little thing, if you like the type, but there's absolutely nothing upstairs but straw. How could you be happy with *that*!?"

The prince laughed long and loud.

"Big sister," he said, "our standards for potential mates are a wee bit different. I think the Princess Rosanna will suit me quite well, thank you, and more to the point, so will the Kingdom of Mährenia that comes with her. And, should I find her company less palatable than that of my worthy sister here, we'll just dwell in separate quarters, and I'll spend my time associating with someone else more to my liking."

"*Mährenia?*" Arrhiána smiled. "You want to *live* in Mährenia? You might as well fall off the edge of the earth. I hear they still ride cows there."

"Then I'll show them what bulls are for. Or headstrong princesses!"

He smiled again.

His sister blushed a bright red, nearly as bright as the cap on her head.

"Enough of that now, Nicky," she said. "It's clearly time for you to go. But do take care, brother. And watch over Papá and Kásha for me."

On an impulse, she pulled the feather from her cap and tucked it carefully into the strap of his helmet.

"That's an easy promise to keep, Rhie," Nikolaí said, kissing her gently on the forehead. "Be kind, lovely sister."

He stepped back and looked her over, as if wanting to impress the memory of her golden hair and bright blue eyes deep into his soul. Then he turned, mounted his horse with a jangle of spurs, adjusted his helmet so the feather was cocked at a jaunty angle, grinned his boyish, lopsided smile, and back over his shoulder tossed the words: "Remember me!" before riding up the boulevard to the palace.

She never forgot that day as long as she lived.

CHAPTER ELEVEN
"AN INTERESTING CONCLUSION"

That evening, Otakar Count of Myláßgorod hosted a celebratory banquet to honor the king and his sons, the high councilors of state, and the officers of the Royal Army. The hall of the citadel was not nearly as large or sumptuous as that of Tighrishály Palace in Paltyrrha, and the food served there, while palatable, certainly not as well prepared, but both seemed like paradise to men who had been living on the road for several weeks, and who knew full well that this was likely to be the last civilized meal that they would consume for months.

Count Otakar was a sour-faced little man of some forty-five years. Nothing in life had ever pleased him except the acquisition of money, of which he had extorted more than his fair share from his unwilling peasants and noblemen. He had never married—the wags insisting that he'd never found a dowry large enough or a woman small enough to suit him—and so his heir was his boisterous cousin, Lord Zygmunt, who sat immediately to his right, as was his due, but to whom the count never deigned to speak a word during the entire meal.

Instead, Otakar drank flagon after flagon of cheap vinegary wine, growing increasingly dour as the evening wore on, and his guests consumed more and more of his precious food and drink.

Finally, he rose dutifully to his feet.

"A toast!" he squeaked, his flinty little eyes darting about the musty old hall. "I give you Kyprianos, King of Kórynthia and

Overlord of Pommerelia!"

"King Kipriyán!" the lords all exclaimed, downing yet another round of drinks.

One could almost see Otakar toting up his expenses, cup by cup.

The king stood in turn to offer a counter-toast, to "Otakar, Count of Myláßgorod and Lord of Bölha!"

And they drank to that and to fifteen other worthies.

Otakar groaned out loud. *This will bankrupt me*, he thought to himself, even though he had purchased the cheapest provisions that he could find. He quietly burped, and rubbed the dull pain in his belly. *Maybe too cheap*, he thought. He had a terrible *gyomorrontás* of the stomach.

No one paid any attention to the count, though, until he suddenly slumped over into his cousin's lap. Lord Zygmunt angrily tried to push him away, before belatedly realizing that something was seriously wrong with Otakar.

"Help!" he yelled. "Help! I need a doctor here!"

Fra Jánisar offered his services immediately, but quickly realized he was too late.

"Count Otakar is dead!" he said.

"Dead!" The word flitted around the room from nobleman to soldier, like a bee buzzing from flower to flower.

"Dead!" The whispering never seemed to stop.

Arkády immediately took charge of the situation, pulling Jánisar to one side.

"What is it?" he asked quietly.

"Poison, I'd say, from the look of him," the doctor said. "Can't be too sure unless I cut him open, but my gut tells me poison."

"Then keep this to yourself," the prince ordered.

"Of course," Jánisar said. "What do you want me to do with him?"

"Let his heir handle the arrangements," Arkády said. "I don't want any cutting on the body. Officially, this will be considered a natural passing. Unbalanced humors, heart, whatever. I'll report the real cause privily to the king."

"Very well, Highness," the physician said, grumbling, and went back to his late patient.

But Prince Arkády had no intention of telling his father what had really happened, for fear of what it might do to the king's confidence. Instead, he carefully reviewed what he knew of the situation, and decided that one of three things must be true. Either Zygmunt had determined to move up his accession date by ten or twenty years, or one of the count's subjects had thought to get an early tax rebate, or their insane killer was involved. But this was a straightforward murder, caused by the insertion of a physical medium into Otakar's food or drink, and so it might actually be traceable.

Arkády quietly ordered the count's plates, cups, and utensils sequestered, sending them to Jánisar for later examination. He also had the servants, servers, and nearby chairmates of Otakar questioned by experienced Psairothi, and decided to interrogate Zygmunt himself.

The new Count of Myláßgorod was happily receiving the condolences of his equally happy subjects, and assuring them that, yes, the tax burden would be eased a bit, a *little* bit, in the very near future, which made them pleased with the quick transition of government. Arkády groaned to himself: any of them would have had considerable justification for wishing Otakar buried deep within his grave.

"Count Zygmunt," the prince said, "I wonder if I might see you for a moment?"

When the count motioned his new friends and supporters to one side, Arkády added a little more forcefully: "Privily, if you please."

Zygmunt shrugged, and begging pardon from his guests, led the prince, accompanied by several of his guards, out of the main hall down a dingy corridor, and into the late count's more intimate reception salon.

Arkády glanced around the dark-paneled room, which was rather plainly adorned with a set of old, faded, and somewhat threadbare tapestries. The tattered hangings had obviously been there for some time, their once brilliant colors now bedimmed with grime and neglect.

Zygmunt gave instructions to the men at the door that they were not to be disturbed.

Arkády wandered over to one of the hangings, and looked at it more closely, shaking his head in disbelief.

"This is one of Jaél's pieces!" he said, as Zygmunt turned back into the room. "They depict the ancient flight of the Psairothi from Atlantis, and the subsequent sinking of that continent beneath the waves. If they were cleaned, they'd be priceless!"

The prince gazed at them in wonder.

"There's not more than a dozen of his tapestries known to exist. We only have one at Tighrishály, and here you have a whole room full of them! See"—he said, pointing to the shield carried by one of the warrior kings of Atlantis—"note the scarab symbol. Jaél used it to mark all of his work."

Arkády then walked around the room, looking at each of the coverings individually.

"Why, they tell the whole story of our race," he said further. "Jaél is supposed to have been another descendent of Mikhaêl Dêmotês Phôstêridês, the founder of the Tighris line and all of our world."

"I had no idea of their value, Highness." The new count yawned, trying not to show his utter lack of interest. He brightened with a sudden thought.

"You're certainly welcome to have them if they would mean something to you," he said. "I intend to refurbish this entire building, and I would probably be disposing of them in any case."

And it couldn't hurt to do the king's son a service, Zygmunt reflected, *now that he was moving up in the world himself.*

"Done!" Arkády said. "Save them for me and I'll see that they're removed to Paltyrrha for restoration as soon as possible."

He cleared his throat.

"However, I need to talk you about something more urgent," the prince continued. "I had your cousin's body examined by the king's physician, Fra Jánisar Cantárian, and he came to an interesting conclusion. Count Otakar was poisoned."

"Wh-what!"

If Zygmunt was faking his astonishment, Arkády was unable to detect it.

"Why, I had no idea," the count said.

He put out a shaky hand and grasped the corner of a nearby desk to steady himself.

Arkády looked him sternly in the eye.

"You understand that we must be sure of what happened," he said, "and yet there must be absolutely no hint of scandal breathed about this anywhere. So what I tell you here today must remain a secret."

"I, uh, I *swear*, Highness."

Zygmunt clearly saw the implications, and just as clearly wanted nothing to do with them.

"Anything you say," he said.

"...And we *must* be certain," the prince said. "Therefore, I request permission to touch your thoughts, to ensure that you had nothing to do with your cousin's untimely passing. You do understand the reasons."

Arkády could see the count visibly gulp with nervousness, as he weighed his alternatives.

"I'll do whatever you want, Highness," Zygmunt said.

"Very well, then," Arkády said. "Just relax, and let me touch your forehead with my *psai*-ring, *so!*"

As he spoke, Arkády dove in swiftly, thoroughly exploring the man's mind, but found nothing very deep there, certainly nothing out of sorts, other than the usual banalities and conceits common to most men. He was amused to confirm that Zygmunt had long dreamed of succeeding to his present position, but had absolutely no idea of what to do with his new-found power, now that he had suddenly acquired it.

"I'm satisfied," the prince said, withdrawing his mind from the other's thoughts. "Now, tell me what you remember of Otakar's actions before the banquet."

But try as he might, Zygmunt could contribute nothing of value to the investigation, since he had had little to do with his cousin on a daily basis; quite the contrary, they had avoided each other very deliberately. Arkády finally gave up and dismissed the much relieved nobleman, assuring him that he would have no further need of his services that day.

CHAPTER TWELVE
"WHY ARE YOU TORMENTING ME?"

Later that evening the prince received a more detailed report from Fra Jánisar. He was dismayed to hear that a telltale had indeed been recovered in the mind of one of the serving boys, who had obviously been compelled to put a drop of something lethal into Otakar's cup before giving it to him.

"What can you tell me about the poison?" Arkády asked.

"Common stuff," Jánisar said. "The murderer could have acquired it almost anywhere in the local area, could have distilled it himself, in point of fact, with a little knowledge and some equipment, which I'm convinced he had. No, there's nothing here that will lead us to anyone else. Once again he's covered his tracks completely."

"We're not getting anywhere with this, Ján," the prince said, combing his fingers through his hair in frustration. "We're always forced to react to things, we never initiate them. The killer's always one step ahead of us. Is there anything we can do to draw him out?"

The physician sighed deeply.

"Without knowing the motivations for his actions," he said, "we're rather like that tiny ant you see there on the floor"—he pointed with his thumb to one of the parquet squares—"who wanders around in loops and in circles, endlessly questing, but knowing not what he seeks, until at last he happens upon a dead beetle or a crumb of food. Then he'll mark the spot and hurry on back to his mates, so they can join the feast.

"We're also running to and fro in aimless meanderings, and we'll continue to do so unless we can think our way out of this conundrum by somehow 'rising above the floor,' thus gaining a new perspective, or until we stumble upon the 'crumb' of knowledge."

The doctor stood up, scratched his head, and yawned wearily.

"Well, let me think about the problem and report back to you," Jánisar said. "I have an idea that might work, but I need to check on something first."

"And I need to get back to my men tonight," the prince said. "I'm sorry for keeping you so late."

As he turned to leave, he accidentally stepped on the ant, utterly crushing it and the bit of food it carried.

Arkády had decided on their arrival that morning that he would not remain with Kipriyán and the other officers in the citadel, as attractive an option as that might be. Someone had to watch over the nearby camp, and the king was better left to his rest in the castle.

When he reached his tent, the prince quickly called for Father Athanasios, and ordered him to take down a letter to be delivered to Princess Arrhiána in Paltyrrha. As he dictated, he reviewed the events of the day. It was obvious to him that their mysterious tormentor was still at work, and that he had traveled with them all the way from the capital. That fact reduced the number of possibilities considerably, unless he was an outsider, which the prince greatly doubted.

"'Further'," Arkády dictated, "'I am convinced that the intent of the killer is not just to disrupt the workings of the court, but to instill a malaise into the very heart of the government itself. These acts are intended to humiliate all or some of us, and in the process to generate chaos. I am filled with the greatest forebodings, dear sister, and I ask you to pray most earnestly for our father, for your brothers, and for this, our enterprise'."

Arkády indicated with a sweep of his hand that he was finished.

"Sign it as usual, if you please, and drop it into the dispatch pouch for delivery tonight."

"Yes, highness," the archpriest said, and bowed gracefully before withdrawing.

The monk did not comment about the news Arkády was sending to his sister, and for that, the prince was profoundly grateful. Then he checked the picket lines once more, and surveyed the peaceful camp full of snoring soldiers wrapped in their bedrolls. Dismissing his aides, he prepared himself for bed, and hoped he would be able to sleep in spite of the thoughts churning through his head. As he drifted off, he heard a voice—perhaps it was his own—crying out, "God help us. God help us all!"

* * * * * * *

Meanwhile, in his apartment within the citadel, King Kipriyán was still pacing the floor, nearly beside himself with fear and anguish. Another one of his nobles had died under mysterious circumstances.

"Why?" the monarch cried out repeatedly. "Why me?"

Doctor Melanthrix paced along with him, trying to calm his master's terror.

"Perhaps the attack was not directed at you, majesty," the philosopher said. "The Count Otakar was not a popular man, and he undoubtedly had many enemies...."

"But *you've* always told me that the Dark-Haired Man is behind this vendetta," the king said.

"True," the philosopher said. "However, we are not convinced that this is one of those occasions."

Now he led the king toward the huge gilt bed piled high with feather-filled comforters.

"You will sleep much better if you drink one of my potions," Melanthrix said, "and in the morning, you will feel yourself again. Please, Highness," he urged, pushing the silver phial towards the king's trembling lips.

"Oh, very well," Kipriyán said, grimacing as he forced down the evil-smelling brew.

"Where do you *get* this foul stuff?" he grumbled.

"Our ingredients are both rare and pure, majesty," Melanthrix said, "but for you, they represent our especial gift, our little contribution to the health of the state."

He watched closely as Kipriyán's eyes began to flutter.

"Now we see you becoming drowsy," he said. "Very good. Just lie back upon your bed, and let the mist take you. You will feel rested on the morrow, and none of these cares will seem quite as awful then. Just sleep."

He gently pulled the linen coverlet over the loudly-snoring king, blew out the beeswax taper by the bed, and watched, lost in thought, as the smoke curled up towards the rafters. Then, like a ghost, Melanthrix drifted quietly out of the room, and was gone.

But the king of Kórynthia slept restlessly that night, bedeviled by dreams of the Dark-Haired Man, whose shaggy form kept stalking and killing his family and his friends one by one.

"What are you doing to me?" he cried out in his anguish. "Why are you tormenting me?"

CHAPTER THIRTEEN
"THE MAN HAD A BAD STOMACH"

On the next morning, the Feast of Saint Ktêsiphôn, a solemn memorial mass was held in the ancient Cathedral of Saint Stachys the Apostle at Myláßgorod, for the repose of the soul of Otakar late Count of that region. Presiding over the service was Metropolitan Ismaêl, who had transited from Paltyrrha early that morning; he was assisted by the frail and elderly Patriarch Avraäm. Many present remarked on the latter's haggard demeanor.

Since this was Ismaêl's see, however, it was appropriate that he give the homily, and so he began:

"My Lord King, Most Holy Patriarch, my lords spiritual and temporal, I come to praise a man who was ever dutiful to his king, and who paid his tithe to the church most regularly. He was never one to seek the flattery or praise of other men, nor did he...."

And he droned on and on in that fashion interminably, like a honey-laden bee floating lazily on the breeze, while many of the older members of the congregation began fidgeting and shifting their weight from one foot to another, trying to find a comfortable position. They stood in rows according to rank in the crowded little cathedral, with the king and his sons and the metropolitans of the church in the first range nearest the altar, and the others bunched up uncomfortably behind them.

Ismaêl was relating a remarkably tedious anecdote about the late count's little-known and -appreciated acts of charity, which none present had ever witnessed or noticed, when he paused, swallowed heavily, a look of puzzlement suddenly coming over his beefy face, and abruptly keeled over dead.

Metropolitan Timotheos rushed over to his colleague, felt for an absent pulse, and began giving him the last rites. The old patriarch began to sob inconsolably, and had to be led away to his quarters by Archpriest Athanasios. The king's face progressively went white with shock, then red with anger, that the sanctity of the church should be so blatantly violated.

"Find out what happened," he said to Prince Arkády.

"At once, sire," the prince said, his own mind reeling.

Fra Jánisar, the king's physician, was already running to the body, which he began examining as soon as Timotheos was finished administering the sacrament. Arkády ordered the guards to clear the area so the doctor could work.

Jánisar motioned with his hand to Arkády.

"I want to show you something," he said.

He pulled back the right sleeve of Ismaêl's vestment. "See here?" The physician pointed to a small red dot just above the metropolitan's elbow.

"What is it?" Arkády asked.

"A bite, perhaps," Janiser said, "or maybe the prick of a needle. I've noticed something similar on two of the other bodies, and I suspect it was present on some of the earlier ones, as well. Perhaps a serum or drug is injected by the attacker to weaken the victim's resistance to a mental probe. This direct physical contact may be a necessary prelude to whatever he eventually does with their minds."

The prince examined the arm more closely.

"What about Otakar's body?"

The Doctor shook his gray head.

"After considering the circumstances, I find nothing similar in the way the count died to the attacks we've been experiencing against members of the court."

"Can you isolate the substance from this new attack?" the prince asked.

"No," came the reply. "I have no means of identifying the drug without a usable sample, and even then, I strongly suspect it's something I've never seen before. I don't know of any Psairothi potion that would have precisely this effect. However, whenever we return to Paltyrrha, I'll be able to consult with several of my colleagues in the east. They may have some better idea of what this is and how it can be countered."

"What else can you tell me?" asked Arkády.

"Well," the doctor said, sighing, "I still believe that the individual involved is one of us. The methodology being employed suggests that some kind of personal contact between killer and victim is essential to the perpetration of these crimes. That in turn implies regular access to the king and his councilors, a knowledge of official etiquette that is fairly sophisticated, and the ability to appear non-threatening or at least familiar to everyone at court."

"Then...." the prince blurted out.

"*Yes!*" Jánisar said, "absolutely yes. The victims all knew their murderer. I don't know what frightens me more, the idea of some monster harvesting us like so many helpless sheep, or the fact that somebody at court is at this moment methodically planning the destruction of his next target."

He gazed down at the inert body of Metropolitan Ismaêl.

Arkády shuddered.

"Ján, you mentioned earlier today that you had a plan...."

"Just an idea, Highness," the doctor said. "I haven't worked it out completely yet."

He snorted, and nodded his head at the body.

"Too much to do, sire. Just give me a few days. Please."

"Very well," the prince said. "Do your usual necroprobe, not that I expect it to tell us anything more than before. And keep quiet about this, if you will."

"Of course, sir," Jánisar said.

Arkády returned to the king. "Biliousness," he muttered. "The man had a bad stomach."

No one much believed him.

CHAPTER FOURTEEN
"THE DARK FIRST, AND THEN THE LIGHT"

That same morning at Tighrishály Palace in Paltyrrha, the Princess Dúra was comfortably seated in a sunny corner of the solar with several of her ladies, knitting a shawl for Queen Brisquayne's new great-grandchild, when one of her maids came dashing in unannounced.

"It's Prince Ari!" she screamed, as the women looked up in surprise. "Come quickly, princess!"

Dúra dropped the shawl and ran out of the solar as fast as her short, plump legs could carry her. Prince Arkády's quarters were located several floors above, and she was perspiring and breathless by the time she reached the entrance to their apartment. Even before she entered, she could hear the pitiful moans of her son.

"Oh, God," she prayed, steadying herself for the worst, "please give him life. Please take away his pain."

As she entered the children's rooms, she immediately looked for the signal bell in its customary place, but it was nowhere to be seen, and she frantically began to scan the room for it, impatiently pushing away her eldest daughter, who was pulling at her sleeve to get her attention.

"Mamá, Mamá!" Rÿna cried out, "I rang the bell already. I'm sorry, Mamá, but it called out to me, and I sent for Melánty. He's on his way, I'm sure of it."

Dúra finally understood what her daughter was trying to

tell her, and bent down and hugged her close, kissing away the frantic tears.

"It's all right, little one," she murmured. "You did well."

Then Dúra turned to her son, and took his hand in hers, trying to comfort him while they waited. It seemed as if an eternity passed before the shadowy figure of Doctor Melanthrix finally appeared at the doorway.

"We heard Rÿna call," he whispered, "and so we came as quickly as possible. My dear boy," he said, hurrying to the young prince lying pain-wracked in his feather bed, "whatever do we have here? My poor, poor lad. We brought you your medication. This will make you feel a bit better."

Then he forced a drop of the liquid down Prince Arión's throat.

After the boy had fallen into a deep sleep, Doctor Melanthrix sat back, his face creased with lines of weariness.

"My dear lady," he said, "we may not be available regularly in the future, due to prevailing conditions in the west, and so we must instruct you in the use of this preventative. There are two classes of elixir, one dark, one light. When the boy suffers one of these attacks, give him two drops—*no more, mind!*—of the dark, until he sleeps. When he wakes, give him one sip of the light, and another later that same day, at about the dinner hour. Then he will recover from the spell."

"What about the needles?" she asked.

"He has passed the point where that technique might prove effective," the old philosopher said. "What we have supplied you with now will last you for some months, and we shall replenish the stock when we return from battle. There is no permanent cure for this affliction, although the attacks will diminish when he finally reaches adolescence."

"Will he live?" Dúra asked.

"Who can say, madame, who can say?" the old philosopher said. "'Man born of woman has but a short life to live,' sayeth the Scripture. All of those whom we knew in our youth are gone now, save one or two. This much only can we say, that your son will not perish from this illness. Of that you may rest assured. Now, we must depart. Remember: the dark first and then the light."

She thought to ask him something else, and hurried to the corridor after the man, but he was nowhere to be found, despite the fact that he had just exited the room. When she returned to Ari's side, Princess Grigorÿna was seated near her brother, still holding the silver bell in her right hand.

"Rÿna," her mother said.

"Yes, Mamá," the girl said.

"I love you very much, my first-born child." Dúra smiled. "I've decided to make you the official Custodian of the Bell. We shall keep it here, of course, in case you're playing outside when it's needed. But when you're here, *you* shall be the one to ring it, and no one else."

Rÿna was beside herself with joy. The bell seemed part of her now, and she couldn't imagine being without it.

"Did you hear that, Ouisa?" she told her old rag doll a little later. "I'm the chief bellkeeper now."

"Oh yes, dear Rÿna," Louisa said. "And it's such a lovely bell, too, isn't it? We'll keep it with us always."

CHAPTER FIFTEEN
"FOR KING KIPRIYÁN
AND KÓRYNTHIA!"

Shortly after midnight on the morrow, the Feast of Saint Pêrêgrinos the Beknighted, Prince Nikolaí gathered an elite squad of two hundred of the King's Rangers, and led the way out of Myláßgorod Camp. A few miles north of town, they turned to follow the Liyépaya Fork of the Myláß River, as it slowly entered the eastern flank of the Carpates or Trans-Oxian Mountains. They met the scout Sir Léka d'Örs at the base of the Skopélosz Pass.

"Highness!" Sir Léka saluted.

"Is everything ready?" Nikolaí asked.

"I have the extra horses here," the scout said, motioning to a line of mounts tethered to one side.

"Then let's proceed," the prince said, turning and shouting to his men: *"For King Kipriyán and Kórynthia!"*

"For King Kipriyán and Kórynthia!" two hundred voices agreed.

Each of the rangers grabbed the reins of another horse, and trailed it behind him. Then the troop started up Skopélosz Road at a trot, led by Sir Léka and Prince Nikolaí. The light of the half-moon was more than sufficient to show them the way, and they proceeded rapidly up the slight incline.

The valley of the Liyépaya was broad and easily traversed, even during flood season. One permanent stone bridge was located near the bottom of the canyon to assist the traveler over the widest part of the river, and beyond that point several easy fords were passable much of the year 'round.

Each of the soldiers changed mounts at the halfway point. A little further along the gorge the river split again, and once more they took the left-hand branch, now reduced to a mere creek, called the Corgátha. Their well-defined road proceeded southwest through the mountains, bypassing a series of green meadows covered with beaver ponds. The way was fringed on either side with blueberry bushes, ferns, and the hulks of giant evergreens. Occasionally they would hear a deer bounding away, or an owl hooting in the distance, or a night hawk calling at them as it circled in the cold air high above.

Near the top of the pass the air became crisp and cool, and they could see the breaths of their horses snorting out in front of them. They dismounted a few hundred yards short of the summit, where a small strongpoint, called Fort Bürnhoff by the Kórynthis, was located, and proceeded the rest of the way on foot. Sir Léka quietly pointed out the weaknesses that he had scouted some days before, and then Prince Nikolaí took command, using ring-glow signals to deploy his men around the poorly-guarded structure.

The archers carefully notched their arrows, holding several others at the ready; at the prince's mark, they silently began dropping the Pommerelian guards patroling the wooden palisades some ten feet above them, shooting as fast as they could draw. All died quietly, and no alarum was given.

Then, a specially trained squad used knotted ropes to catch the pointed wood posts making up the outer wall of the fort, and the rangers quickly pulled themselves up and over, silently invading the compound, like an army of ghosts capturing a long-dead ruin.

It was all over within moments. Most of the defenders were surprised in their bedrolls, and never even had a chance to draw their weapons before they were confronted with long, pointed blades at their throats. The majority surrendered without even being asked.

"What are our casualties?" Nikolaí asked.

"Two dead, eleven wounded," Sir Léka said.

"And the enemy?"

"At least forty dead, about the same number wounded, and over two hundred taken prisoner."

"Then post our standard," the prince said, and watched as the crouching ochre tiger of his house was raised over the eastern gate, just in time for the first light from the rising sun to catch its fluttering waves.

"Sir Léka," he continued, "I want you to ride to the king, and report that Fort Kipriyán has been taken."

There was a rousing cheer all around as the men heard the name of their rechristened fort.

"Sir Yáros," he added, "take ten men down the west side of the pass into Borgo Canyon, check the approaches to Borgösha, and warn us of any reinforcements being sent up the mountain."

"Yes, sir," both men echoed, and rushed to their respective duties.

The rangers had just captured the only obstacle blocking Kórynthi access to the city of Borgösha.

Meanwhile, the main army was preparing to depart its camp outside Myláßgorod. The previous afternoon, King Kipriyán had confirmed the new Count Zygmunt in his rank, accepting his obeisance, and then ordered him to remain at home. Someone had to be present there to organize the reinforcements coming from other parts of the kingdom, including the much-delayed Arrhéni Brigade.

At the same time, Patriarch Avraäm had appointed Timotheos, the Metropolitan of Örtenburg and All Nördmark, as the new *Locum Tenens* of the Holy Church to replace the deceased Ismaêl; he had already returned to Paltyrrha to assume his office.

The largest military force ever assembled in Kórynthia moved out of camp not long after sunrise, heading towards the same pass traversed by the rangers earlier that day. Shortly after they entered the canyon, a horseman was spotted riding fast down the road. Several men drew their weapons until they recognized the familiar face of Sir Léka. He was immediately escorted to the king.

"Sire," he said, "I have the great pleasure to announce that Prince Nikolaí has taken Fort Kipriyán, and is waiting for you at the top of the pass."

The news swept the army instantly, prompting spontaneous cheers up and down the line. All of the seasoned soldiers knew that Borgösha was dominated by the heights, and control of the pass ultimately meant control of the city. They proceeded up Skopélosz Road with renewed vigor.

About that same time, the Pommerelian commander in Borgösha, Gajus Count Thulden, sent a supply wagon with twenty guards up the road through Borgo Canyon to Fort Bürnhoff. They never returned. Late in the afternoon, having become concerned by the lack of communication, the count dispatched an experienced scout named Claret to investigate. He quietly reached his destination after dark, heard the enemy soldiers enjoying the provisions that the Pommerelians had so generously donated to them, and just as silently withdrew, making his report to his master later that night, after moonrise.

CHAPTER SIXTEEN
"LAST NIGHT I DREAMT I WENT TO KÓRYNTHÁLY AGAIN"

It took two full days for the initial units of the Kórynthi force to traverse the Skopélosz Pass, and another to assemble five great catapults on the heights jutting out over the city, where they perched like a row of giant mantises ready to feast on their defenseless victims.

On the morning of the Feast of Saint Poudentiana, they began lobbing huge stones over the city walls of Borgösha, smashing soldiers and civilians alike, together with their animals, houses, wagons, and anything else that got in the way. Count Gajus could do nothing. Indeed, while he was inspecting the battlements in mid-afternoon, he was suddenly crushed by one of the giant rocks, together with several of his officers and advisors. His unexpected passing utterly demoralized the defenders.

On the morning of the twentieth day of May, the Feast of Saint Vasilla, Borgösha was abandoned by the army of Pommerelia. A half-hearted attempt to burn the citadel was extinguished by the townsmen who chose to remain, and the gates of the city were thrown open to the invaders.

King Kipriyán promptly accepted the gift.

At the hour of *hektê* the first regiments of the Kórynthi force began entering the city in columns of four, deploying rapidly throughout the streets. Squads were dispatched to clean up the *débris* caused by the recent bombardment. After the King's Guard had taken their positions, the town was thoroughly searched by trained Psairothi for spies and sympathizers to the Pommerelian cause. These were executed where they were found, together with any family members associated with them, and their heads posted on pikes along the city walls. The row of blankly-staring faces seemed to work wonders for the maintenance of discipline.

Outside the town the rest of the army began setting up camp, with units being dispatched in all directions to scout the region, requisition foodstuffs, and provide advance warning of any attacks from local partisans or the remnants of Thulden's army. The nearby farmers proved most willing to contribute to the cause, particularly when prompted by the possible drafting of their sons into the army or their daughters into the officers' bedchambers. It took five full days to get the entire Kórynthi force over the mountains and organized back into some semblance of a military structure.

King Kipriyán ordered a ceremony to be held later that afternoon in the main square of Borgösha, to establish an official government for the region. At the hour of *enatê*, which is called *none* in the west, Kipriyán again proclaimed Humfried v the rightful King of Pommerelia, and placed upon his head a thin golden crown. Humfried in turn bowed his knee before King Kipriyán, and officially and publicly acknowledged him as overlord of the kingdom. Humfried's absent son, Prince Pankratz, was then declared Hereditary Prince by his father, who also created him Duke of Balíxira. The father of the new king, Prince Ezzö, was given the additional title of Duke of Einwegflasche. General Rónai was ennobled as Lord of Borgösha, and General Reményi as Lord of Karkára.

As Humfried started to work through a long scroll detailing the awards and honors to be granted to his now numerous supporters and followers, a storm began building back over the spine of the Carpates Range, a common enough occurrence in these parts during the warm afternoons of the spring and summer months. Distant grumblings were soon filtering down over the foothills. As Humfried droned on with his cloying statements of self-congratulation, the skies continued to blacken, and Prince Arkády nudged his father to get his attention.

"Sire," he whispered, "it's going to rain soon. Shouldn't we retire to the main hall?"

But King Kipriyán waved his hand for silence and patience, even when the first few heavy drops peppered Humfried's document, realizing full well that to leave out even the minor awards might pique some of the new monarch's instant entourage.

Overhead the thunder kept coming ever closer, and the light kept growing ever dimmer. A sharp wind began whirling through the square, blowing the robes of the clerics this way and that.

"Humfried," Kipriyán shouted, "perhaps you'd better complete this quickly."

"Yes, *Cousin*," the new king said, rolling up the scroll.

Suddenly, a brilliant white flash illuminated the entire area, as the great elm in the center of the square was struck by lightning. A dozen men were blown into the air, and another score or so knocked completely senseless. A falling limb crushed two of them where they lay.

"The king!" somebody shouted, and Prince Arkády turned to his left to find his father stretched out unconscious upon the ground. The monstrous branch of the tree had missed his head by inches.

"We need a doctor here!" the prince shouted.

When no one responded, he looked wildly around the square, trying to find Fra Jánisar, but the rain then decided to come down in earnest, compounding the mess before him. He could see nothing.

Nikolaí suddenly appeared on the other side of the king.

"Does he live? Where's the physician?" he shouted above the roar of the storm.

"Yes, he lives. I don't know where Jánisar is," Arkády yelled back. "See if you can find him."

Right behind them a squad of guards were trying to move the heavy branch that had almost caught the king.

"Oh, God," Nikolaí groaned.

Arkády turned to see a bejeweled hand sticking out from underneath the limb, and shook his head in disbelief.

"Oh, Ján," he mumbled. "Not you, too!"

"We can help," someone said from behind Nikolaí.

They turned back towards the king to see Doctor Melanthrix standing before them, his multicolored robes soaked through, his packet of potions grasped firmly in his left hand.

"We can help," the philosopher said again.

"Then do so!" Arkády ordered.

"Just a moment. What are you doing, Kásha?" Nikolaí asked, but shrank back when he saw his brother's face.

Melanthrix knelt next to the body of Kipriyán, fumbled in his leather bag, and brought out a small green bottle that seemed twisted around itself. There was no stopper to undo. Instead, the philosopher inserted the end of the phial into the king's mouth, muttered a few words, and waited. The bottle flashed briefly a brilliant emerald, sparkling like a jewel.

Kipriyán stirred and opened his eyes. "What happened?" he asked.

"Praise God!" Arkády said, crossing himself.

Nikolaí did the same.

"Last night I dreamt I went to Kórynthály again," Kipriyán whispered.

"What?" Arkády said.

The Princes Kiríll and Zakháry rushed over, and yanked Melanthrix away from their father.

"Charlatan!" Zakháry yelled. "Keep your unclean hands off of him."

The philosopher shook them off, like a dog shedding the rain, and straightened himself to his full height, trying to arrange his wet, bedraggled robes.

"Do not touch *us* again," he hissed, water dripping from his long white nose.

"Zack, Kir," Arkády said, "he just saved father's life."

"I don't like him," Zakháry said. "He's warped father's

mind."

"My friend," the king gasped. "He's *my* friend. Mine!"

"See what I mean?" Zakháry said. "Quack!" he shouted, while Kiríll led the philosopher away. "Quack, quack, quack!"

"Come, sire, let's go inside," Arkády urged, and with Nikolaí's help got the old king to his feet.

The ceremony was over.

CHAPTER SEVENTEEN
"IT'S *JIHAD!*"

On this same day, Prince Ezzö and his grandson, Hereditary Prince Pankratz, were preparing to invade Einwegflasche through the Kultúra Pass in western Bolémia. They had gathered their eight thousand soldiers and mercenaries at Castle Körösladány on the east end of the canyon, which was formed by the entrance of the Kultúra River into the Royánna Mountains just south of Mount Töpöl. Also present there in order to give them the stirrup cup and bid them *bonne chance* were Ezzö's sisters, the Princesses Arizélla and Ezzölla, his wife, Princess Teréza, Pankratz's wife, Hereditary Princess Minérva, and King Humfried's wife and daughter, Queen Pulkhériya and Princess Salentína.

"Pánky, isn't this just *grand*!" his stepmother sang out with delight, stretching out her scrawny neck as she gazed about the courtyard at the colorful display of troops gathered there. She was soon joined by her prissy, simpering daughter-in-law, Nérva, who was technically in mourning, and her equally scrawny ten-year-old daughter, Tína.

Pankratz, in the midst of final preparations for this, his cross-cultural adventure, was making a mighty effort to ignore the women's comments, albeit unsuccessfully.

Off to one side, the Princess Arizélla had cornered her younger brother, and was speaking earnestly with him, punctuating her words with grimaces and gestures. One graying strand of hair strayed fetchingly across her cheek, as she shook her head vigorously.

"Ezzösh, don't go," she said. "I know you're not yourself, and you know as well as I that you can do nothing to help this, this *cause* of Humfried."

She reached out and took his gnarled hand tenderly in her own.

"I must go," he said, his once sparkling eyes now dulled with pain. "Don't you see, I *must* go," he repeated. "It's *jihad!* I...Élla, what's wrong with me?"

"Oh, Ezzösh," was all she could say, her voice choked with emotion. To see her younger brother reduced to a shadow of his former intellect was a torture even beyond death. She kissed him gently on the forehead.

"What are you two old sourpusses up to now?" came the shout of their younger sister, Ezzölla. "Oh, come see the soldiers, Élla! They look so gay in all their finery."

The princess was running about like a young girl again, eyes flashing, and her skirts flying dangerously high.

"God's teeth!" Arizélla muttered to herself, directing her gaze skyward. Was there no end to it? There were times when she could cheerfully strangle her sister.

"Ezzösh?" She turned back to him once more.

"I must go," was all he would say. "*Jihad!*"

"Come, Grandpapá," Prince Pankratz shouted to them from the promenade. "It's time for us to leave."

"Pánky," Pulkhériya said, whining, "please take us with you."

"What?" The prince sat straight up in his saddle, aghast at the suggestion. "Stepmamá, this is no journey for a woman."

"But you yourself have said that it'll all be over in a few weeks," the queen said, "and Tína and I want to see your great victory over the Walküri."

"Me, too," Minérva said. "I want to go, too!"

Her black dress fluttered idly in the wind.

"Now, just a moment," the prince said, putting up his hands as if to ward off an assault. "This isn't going to be a walk in the garden, ladies. There'll be no fine accommodations for anyone, no dainty meals or troubadours or dances or anything else that I know you all enjoy. We'll be sleeping on the ground in tents, and eating cold salted beef and pork. There'll be insects, and it'll be none too clean...."

"I don't mind in the least little bit," Pulkhériya said, pouting. "Things have become so incredibly dull at court, I'd really like to have a little adventure. And just think how surprised your father will be to see me."

"Me, too!" Minérva squeaked her refrain, a little more loudly this time, gaining a withering glance from her disgusted husband for her efforts. She had seemingly forgotten entirely about the death several weeks earlier of little Prince Alexander, her firstborn son.

"Enough!" Pankratz said. "*Enough!* I have other things to worry about. If you want to come so badly, then come, and the Devil be damned. I won't try to stop you, ladies. But I don't want to hear any complaints. Once we've started, there'll be no turning back, not for anyone, not for any reason. That's my final word."

"Oh!" the queen simpered, now that she'd gotten her way.

Her large, yellowish teeth parted in a self-satisfied grin, as she brayed at her unhappy stepson.

"Complain?" she said. "Why, we *never* complain."

She waved her hand at the servants to get her things packed and her carriage ready for departure.

Prince Pankratz just shook his head helplessly. *What else could he do?* he thought, as he directed the ladies and their carriage to the rear of the train. Calling the captain of his personal guard over, he gave him instructions to keep the women in sight at all times.

"At *all* times, Libás," he said. "I want someone watching them at every single moment of the day, even when they go off somewhere to take a piss."

That'll fix them! he thought savagely, as the young officer trotted off to do his bidding.

At midmorning the troop went marching out the main gate of Körösladány, heading up the Kultúra Pass, which is called the Krempesgruft in Pommerelia. The Kultúra River penetrated the mountain range almost to its far side, creating a natural byway that facilitated travel between Bolémia and Einwegflasche, and also serving as a traditional invasion route for both sides. The actual border between Kórynthia and Pommerelia was located at the head of the Pass, near the western flank of the Royánna Mountains, which is called the Dreivan Range in the west.

* * * * * * *

Late in the afternoon of the second day, they reached the border post, situated at the top of a long, slow rise. On the north side of the canyon the spray of a waterfall off the side of the cliff announced the arrival of a new Kultúra. A plain stone wall stretched across the narrow divide, bisected by a wooden gate.

"Halt!" came the command from above.

But the column continued to push forward.

"Halt, I say," came the anonymous call, "or we'll fire."

But the Bolémi soldiers marched right up to the wall with a giant log slung between them, and started beating the door down with their makeshift ram.

A desultory shower of arrows peppered the invaders, killing a few, but mostly sticking in the shields they held above their heads. A couple of additional swings of the log broke the latch-bolt, and the door banged to the ground with a thump.

A great cloud of dust billowed up around them as they rushed through the opening they had created, and systematically swept away the two dozen men acting as guardians of the old culture. No one escaped. The enemy bodies were stripped and dumped in a pile to one side. Sappers began tearing down the wall to either side of the entrance so they could get their machines through.

The army camped there overnight.

Early the next morning the troops marched straight into

Einwegflasche without further opposition, and by the middle of the following day they were investing Lockenlöd Castle, the chief seat of Count Iselin.

CHAPTER EIGHTEEN
"STRANGE WORK OF FATE"

Far to the southwest, the Dowager Queen Brisquayne was thoroughly enjoying her visit with her twin daughters and grandchildren in the Kingdom of Neustria. She was alternating staying at her sons-in-law's estates at Enghieux, twenty miles east of the city of Lavallière on the north side of the Yèble River, and at the Royal Palace in the capital of Sabbedelle.

Her firstborn daughter, Princess Adeléonore, had married Lord Lancelme Soubize, then the Hereditary Count d'Enghieux, a quarter century earlier. A strapping, buxom lass with rosy red cheeks and flashing dark eyes, she had happily whelped ten healthy surviving children for her handsome husband.

The first girl of the litter, the Countess Brislaine, had been married wisely and well to Prince Léobert, the second son of King Tancrède of Neustria, just the previous year, and their firstborn babe would also be the queen's first great-grandchild.

On this particular morning, Brisquayne was curled up cozily on a puffy, flowered chintz settee in the sun-dappled morning room at Enghieux. Opposite her sat her two daughters, Countess Adèle and her younger twin, Lady Sinthe. All three ladies were busily knitting miniscule bonnets, sacques, and wrappers for the prince-to-be. They sipped spicy hot herb tea laced with honey as they worked, and reminisced about old times at home and all the people they had known there.

Balls of pale yarn—pastel blues, yellows, and greens— bounced up and down and jiggled back and forth as the women's needles clicked merrily along. A pair of white, blue-eyed kittens stealthily stalked the yarn, and rolled about on the tiled floor, fighting vicious, pitched battles with each other, their pink tongues flicking, their white teeth clicking, knatch knatch knatch.

Outside the stately, iron-mullioned windows, the queen could see a dozen or so black-and-white spotted cows grazing peacefully on flower-dotted meadows, their bellies heavy with calves-to-be, their teats bloated with milk. Just beyond them wandered a few scattered sheep, their fluffy white lambs gamboling at their sides. Nearby, a bubbling brook wandered through the landscape, running down to the River Yèble a mile or so distant. A pair of fat, gray geese fed happily on the iridescent mayflies and juicy red worms, stretching out their long, slender necks to the sun, honking at everything and nothing in particular.

"So, who's to midwife?" Brisquayne idly asked her eldest daughter, taking another sip of tea. She held up the piece she was knitting for the others to see.

"That's lovely, Mamá," Adèle said, then responded to her question. "Well, you *know* that Queen Hippolyte has insisted on making all of the birthing arrangements herself. Poor Laine has *not* been allowed to do anything to help."

She paused a moment to pull her yarn away from an inquisitive kitten, before continuing.

"They've found some strange old woman from the east to assist with the birthing," she said. "Oh, she comes *very* highly recommended, they tell me, but Mamá!, she wears *le turban*, if you can imagine, and all these odd baubles and beads. And she speaks with this oh-so-stilted accent. *Très très bizarre!* It always leaves me in absolute *stitches* to listen to her 'zheses' and 'zhoses.' Just wait until you hear her. You'll see what I mean."

"And what about the child's name? Have they actually decided on anything yet?" the old queen asked.

To Brisquayne's delighted surprise, her daughter sat back in her comfy, cushioned chair and laughed out loud, rocking back and forth while holding on to her knitting bunched up in her ample lap. Indeed, with her dark hair now streaked with gray, she looked very much like a slightly younger sibling of her own mother, while Sinthe, her real twin, was a paler, more refined version of the maternal mold.

"That depends on who you ask," Adèle said, wiping the tears of laughter from her rosy cheeks. "They've come up with some truly *choice* possibilities, including Tancarde, Artamène, Blancart, and Néron. Of course, Léobert and Laine have their *own* preferences: Léothéric, Chilpéric, Silvain, Macarie (which is *my* choice, of course), and Restif, but I suspect the king and queen will have the final say. They've been told it's a boy."

"So," Brisquayne mused, "another little prince for La Maison d'Albéric." With her teeth she clipped a stray bit of yarn from the lacy blanket she was knitting, and tossed it to the kittens near her slippered foot.

"I wonder what chance *he* has of ever succeeding to the throne?" she added.

"Not much," Adèle snorted. "Remember, Mamá, that Bertie has an older brother, Prince Albéric. Alby may not have married yet, but he surely *will*. His dear mother will see to that."

Brisquayne arched her eyebrows. She sensed a bit of rivalry between her daughter and her granddaughter's mother-in-law. But she knew her place. She would bite her tongue and stay out of it.

"And when will I meet this marvelous midwife?" the dowager queen asked aloud, her needles flying clickety-clack, clickety-clack as they wove back and forth, weaving an intricate pattern of leys into the yarn.

As she drifted, she could picture herself and her two girls working companionably together there in the sunlit room, almost as if she had risen above the *tableau* and was peering down at it. She felt the love flowing out of their hands and their hearts and into the gifts they were creating for the precious child-to-be, the seed of their combined wombs. To her it seemed as if they were all part of some grand cosmic scheme, a chain of eternal women linking their familial past to the future and beyond.

She was suddenly minded of the old story concerning *Les Parques*, The Fates of classical legend, whose spinning and cutting supposedly determined the length of a person's life, and the pain and suffering they would have to experience during their stay on earth.

Ahhh, she thought to herself, *Adèle is obviously Clotho the spinner, Sinthe is Atropos the cutter, and I, why I'm Lachésis the dispenser.*

She chuckled at the conceit.

"Par quel destin faut-il, par quelle étrange loi,..." she murmured, "Strange work of fate past wondering...."

Brisquayne's second-born daughter, Lady Abyssinthe, wife of Lancelme's younger twin brother, Sieur Manassès, had been working away quietly as the other two chatted, glancing from time to time at an ornate old sundial on the lawn outside the window. Now she perked up her pretty, pearl-like ears, and cleared her throat delicately.

"Well, *actually*," she said, a secret little smile twitching at her lips, "they're all coming here to visit this afternoon. The king and queen, I mean. I expect them about midday. I've put together a luncheon of sorts," she added, gesturing towards the windows. "We'll dine *al fresco* on the terrace, I think...."

"Sinthe!" Brisquayne said, dropping her stitches as she rose straight up from her seat. "You foolish little girl, why didn't you tell me earlier? You always did have cheese balls between those ears of yours. Now I've got to go change, and you both do, too," she scolded, glancing about for her work basket.

The kittens, abruptly disturbed from their nap in the sun, scampered away swiftly. The three ladies quickly packed up their things, Sinthe laughing merrily at the consternation she had caused, and Brisquayne and Adèle shaking their heads and muttering mild curses. Then with triple shouts for their maids, off they went to freshen up before the royals made their appearance.

CHAPTER NINETEEN
"JUST A SILLY HEADACHE"

Some hours later, when their honored guests arrived on schedule, Sieur Manassès and his wife were on hand to greet them demurely in the *porte-cochère*. Also forming the impromptu reception line were the Count Lancelme and his wife, the Lady Adeléonore, and the Dowager Queen Brisquayne of Kórynthia. All present bowed and curtsied deeply to one another, as the salutations were announced.

"My Lord King," Manassès said, sweeping his hand in the general direction of the entrance hall. "We welcome you and your lady most heartily to our humble Enghieux."

"The pleasure is all ours, my boy," King Tancrède said, clapping the baron on the shoulder as he led his small party into the reception salon. "Hippolyte and I are looking forward to our stay here. I do hope the fishing is good."

"Indeed, Majesty, I've snagged several large troutfish and one of the walleyed pike just this past week," the *sieur* jabbered away, glad to have found something in common with his illustrious guest.

The monarch expressed much pleasure at the thought of the proposed fishing expedition that afternoon, and then he and the queen courteously renewed their acquaintanceship with Queen Brisquayne, stepping aside to bring forward a short, plump woman who had been waiting discretely in the background.

"But now, my dear lady," Hippolyte said, "let me introduce to you the main reason for our visit here today. Please meet our new midwife, the Lady Mirza, a native of far-off Umm az-Zakkár." She bowed with a flourish.

"Ve have been ever so delighted to made your acqvaintance, kind lady and gentle-man," Mirza said, a warm smile lighting up her friendly round face, somewhat offsetting the jarring gutteral accent.

A bottle green headwrapping was completely intertwined with her steel gray hair in an *outré* design. She bowed to them rather formally.

"Und ve vill be very happy to have brung your daughter to the birth," she added coyly.

Brisquayne's mental defenses immediately snapped into place with a violence that shook her very soul. *She had heard that voice somewhere before!* Even if she couldn't immediately recognize the face, she was certain this was someone from her past, someone she had once known quite well. She squinted at the strange little woman more closely.

"Well, my dear," the dowager queen finally said, outwardly maintaining her normal demeanor, "I am so pleased to meet you at long last. Do tell us all about yourself. Have you been a midwife for very many years?"

She carefully refrained from extending her hand, since they inhabited different social levels.

"In the east," Mirza said, "vhich is the place vherein I vas trainèd, ve take of zese matters concerning the birthing *very* serious. And so ve studies very hard ze zings zat are necessitated for the making of the good birt', and ve applies zese zoughts to ze place at hand, vhich is here."

She smiled toothily again, clearly pleased with her effort at elucidation.

"Then, you've been doing this for some time now?" Brisquayne said, her mind searching the æther for answers.

"Oh, many, many years have I done such zings," Mirza said with pride. "Many—how do you say them?—ten-years."

"Decades," the king said, already tired of this women's nonsense. "They're called decades, my dear."

But Brisquayne was distracted, paying scant attention to the pleasantries floating back and forth among their party. As Sinthe ushered them out to the sheltered *terrazo* and the lovely meal which awaited them there, the queen sifted back through her deepest memories to place that curious voice. There was also something else, something about the way in which the woman handled herself....

Great God in Heaven, she screamed inwardly, as she smiled absently at King Tancrède, *it's Mösza!*

Suddenly the old queen felt very frightened and very much alone. She tightly pinched the fleshy part of her thigh with her left hand, focusing on the sharp pain to avoid losing control of herself.

This is no accident, she thought, *it can't be. She's come here to....*

"*Mamá!*" Adèle said, causing Brisquayne to look up quickly from her untouched plate of cold quail hen. "Mirza was asking you a question."

"My apologies," the dowager queen said. "I seem to have been distracted by the king's charming anecdote."

Tancrède had been regaling the twin brothers with another hoary old fishing tale.

"No, no, no, 'tis all the one and the same." Mirza chuckled. "My mistaken, to be sure. No, honorèd madame, I ask merely vhere is it you be from?"

"Kórynthia," Brisquayne said abruptly.

"Oh, such a very big place is this kingdom of Kórynt'," the midwife said, "much more big than Umm az-Zakkár."

She slurred the "z" and accented the last syllable of her homeland, trilling it off her tongue like the night call of a mockingbird.

"Delighted ve be to meet wit' zee...." She bowed again.

Why are you here? Brisquayne moaned to herself. *Who told you I was here?*

"...*Très important* it is to take the care of ze little ones," Mirza continued without interruption. "So much can happen to ze pretty *bébé*. Hurt he can be, or vorse, if you not careful be."

She beamed at them all.

"Yes," Queen Hippolyte said, "one must be very careful indeed, which is why we're so happy to have *you* here, Madame Mirza. My cousin, Lady Circé, spoke so highly of you."

"Oh," Mirza said, laughing under her breath, "some say she be a *real* vitch, ha ha ha, but me, I find her most accommodate. She talk, talk, talk all ze time, she tell me zings a midvife perhaps should not hear, eh? Ha, ha. I hear nozings, like a good Mirza, but she, she zink I listen, so she send me to you. I say nozings. Better to be listened to, no?"

Brisquayne had the oddest sensation that Mirza (or *Mösza*, she corrected herself), was speaking directly into her own ears, that she was telling her to say nothing about her real identity, either now or later, and punctuating that threat with her evident ability to harm Brisquayne's innocent ones at any time in the future. The dowager queen had never been so terrified in her entire life. Somehow the midwife had discovered that Brisquayne had been gossiping about her in Kórynthály. Somehow she had found her way here. *Why?* What possible harm had she ever done to Mösza?

"Far better, lady," the dowager queen said, smiling a thin, wintry smile. "Now, if you will all excuse me, majesties, I am feeling distinctly unwell, and I must beg your leave to retire early."

She rose to exit, bowing to each in turn.

"Oh no, Mamá," Sinthe said. "Shall I fetch a physician?"

"No, it's nothing, really, just a silly headache." Brisquayne gestured to her temple. "I get them sometimes. I'll try to join you for dinner later."

CHAPTER TWENTY
"MY PRETTY LITTLE PLAYMATES"

Instead of returning to the spacious guestchamber which had been set aside for her, however, Dowager Queen Brisquayne made straight for the family's small *viridaurum* alcove just off the little chapel that serviced Enghieux. She glanced about carefully, as she half-walked, half-ran to the hidden site, to be sure she wasn't seen by anyone. Then, stepping inside, she focused her energies, twisted the leys, and transited directly back to her manor house, Tamásház, in Kórynthály.

"Mokey!" she roared, exiting her private mirror. "Where *are* you, girl?"

After conducting a thorough search of the lofty old house, room by room and floor by floor, the queen finally discovered her errant maid tucked up cozily in the master bedchamber with Luqman, the steward, by her side. They were not asleep.

"My God!" she said, "what in the world are you two doing in here? No, never mind, don't answer that. I can guess."

A redfaced Luqman carefully pulled the blanket all the way up to his scrawny neck. *C'est très difficile* to be dignified when one has been found by one's mistress utterly without covering.

"Uh, Madame, that is, uh, Milady," he said once or twice, "Highness! I, uh, you see, uh, we weren't expecting you back so soon...."

His shaky voice tapered off, leaving a total silence in its wake, as his mistress stood glaring down at the pair, like a shepherdess who has just discovered her wayward sheep.

And they certainly weren't expecting what she did next. The dowager queen stepped forward into the room, boldly grabbed the covering, and yanked it off the bed.

"Madame!" Luqman exclaimed, utterly mortified, struggling unsuccessfully to shield himself with his hands. Emöke squealed like a shoat at the butchering block, desperately hunching her knees up in front of her bare chest. Unfortunately, that move left another, even more crucial portion of her anatomy wholly unprotected.

The queen grabbed both miscreants quickly, taking each of them by a foot, and her mind surged massively up their bodies and into their brains, completely and immediately subduing both their wills to hers.

"Now, my pretty little playmates," she said, "we'll just see what's *really* been going on here."

She ruthlessly shuffled through their helpless minds, sifting their memories like so many grains of sand.

But these were simple minds, she soon realized, wholly concerned with their temporary carnal pleasures and minor household advantages. There were no devious, hidden plots folded away in their tiny brains, no secrets save those of the most banal kind.

"*Néma!*" The queen spat in disgust, releasing them with great disappointment. Neither of them had known a thing about Mösza.

Emöke and Luqman suddenly realized that, first, they were very naked, and second, that their mistress was still standing there glaring down at them.

"*Pah!*" Brisquayne scoffed, as both tried again to cover themselves, "nothing I haven't seen before. Luqman," she said, "as of this day you're dismissed from my service. You will return the place setting from my royal china that you stole, and you will also pay half the wages due you to the church, in atonement for your sins.

"Mokey," she said to the wide-eyed girl shivering before her, "your wages are henceforth reduced by one-third, and you're also returned to garde-robe duty. You will both report to Rövigó at once, and tell him what I have told you. Now, *get out of my bedroom!*" she yelled, and they went scurrying off as fast as their legs could carry them.

Even before they had cleared the doorway, the queen started to laugh out loud, the tears streaming from her eyes. She laughed and laughed until her sides ached. She couldn't remember having seen anything so funny in years. She would have to make certain to return unexpectedly from her other trips again in the future. This would make a good tale to tell around *les échecs* table the next time she met with her small circle of old friends.

Outside, the sun was just beginning to skim the horizon. She stirred herself from her reverie, and hurried back to her private transit mirror. She must return to Neustria before she was missed. As she set her leys for Enghieux, she swore that she would find out who betrayed her. She also took a holy oath to herself, on all that was sacred to her, that never in her lifetime would she allow that thrice-damn'd bitch Mösza to harm any of her precious ones. *Not ever.* No one could threaten her and hers and be allowed to live.

CHAPTER TWENTY-ONE
"ALL IS LOST"

The first day of June, the Feast of Saint Ioustinos the Philosopher of Nablus, found the Kórynthi army encamped in the Lüstern Field, below the city and castle of Karkára, on the western slope of the Carpates Mountains. At least two thousand Pommerelian soldiers held this mountain fortress, which dominated the plains of southern Einwegflasche, and blocked access through the Karkára Cut from the Kórynthi County of Westmark. King Kipriyán had decreed that the citadel must be taken before the army could proceed to its rendezvous with the forces of Prince Ezzö. The threat to their extended supply lines was just too great to leave an army of such size lingering behind them.

For four days they had tried to find the key to the great fortress perched four thousand feet above them, to no avail. The War Council was now debating their next step.

"Sire," Prince Arkády said, "we have several choices. We can ignore this threat"—groans emanated from around the table—"which we all agree is not an option, or we can reduce this citadel forthwith. But we can't afford to wait much longer. The fall of Lockenlöd Castle and the death of Count Iselin mean that the Princes Ezzö and Pankratz will be turning their thrust south within a few days, as soon as they've regrouped. Although we don't have as far to travel, we have a much larger army to move."

"If I may play devil's advocate," Prince Nikolaí said, "I never supported stopping here in the first place."

He looked around the table at the grim faces of each of his comrades, gauging their measure.

"We need to take advantage of the invasion of the west by Duke Ferdinand. For the moment, the Walküre king has been forced to split his army into several groups to fight our various thrusts into his country. If we move fast enough, with or without the Forellës, we can catch them with their belts knotted 'round their knees. As for Karkára, we can bottle them up with a thousand men stationed along the canyon walls."

"It's still too risky," General Lord Rónai said. "We need those supplies...."

"Why?" Nikolaí asked. "If we march quickly, the trains'll never be able to keep up anyway. So we scavenge from the land, just like all armies do. Already our wagons are being picked to pieces by the partisans coming out of the Läuterung Hills to the west, and we can't stop them without detailing most of our force to permanent guard duty. We throw the dice, and we either win or lose. If we win, we have the spoils of a nation to divide amongst us. If we lose, well, there won't be nearly as many mouths to feed on the way back, and everything'll be chaos anyway as we try to withdraw."

The king finally broke his silence by grunting for attention.

"I won't hear of withdrawing," he said, "and we won't leave a substantial force of the enemy nibbling at our rear. We take the castle. Now, tell me how we do it."

He glared back at them all.

"I have an idea," Prince Kiríll said. "I spent some months a few years ago in Westmark, hunting and fishing in the Carpathian foothills, and I know that Karkára is vulnerable to attack from the northeast. Although the main road from Podébrad gives one no particular advantage, there's a little-known trail that follows a southern branch of the Paltyrrh River called the Vá'al to a point just north of the citadel. A small force could come in through this back way, scale the walls undetected, and open the gates to a full-scale assault. I'd be happy to volunteer, since I know the way."

"How long would it take to get this started?" the king asked, obviously quite pleased with his son's initiative.

"A few days at most," the prince said. "I'd have to use your personal *viridaurum* to transit to Myláßgorod, round up enough trained men, and then either ride to Podébrad in Westmark if the roads are dry, or take the whole lot through the mirrors, and get new mounts and gear up north. We could reach there by the fourth of the month, I think."

"So ordered!" the king roared. "Gorázd, settle the arrangements. Kir, make us all proud. We'll be waiting for your signal.

"Now, any other business?" he asked.

They had begun discussing the disposition of troops for the forthcoming attack, when a messenger was abruptly announced. He staggered into the tent, haggard and worn, his face and clothing soiled, his hair sweaty and hanging loose, his helmet and much of his armor gone and his overtunic in tatters.

"Majesty!" he managed to gasp, almost falling over before grabbing the edge of the table. Several men rushed to his aid.

"Something to drink," he said.

"Get that man some wine," Kipriyán ordered, motioning to a servant. "And a stool for him to sit on. Quickly!"

When the messenger had had a few moments to gain control of himself, he looked up from his cup, and they could see the weariness and despair etched in his face.

"Sire," he began again, "all is lost. I...."

He couldn't continue.

"*Who* is lost? Where?" Arkády asked.

The soldier looked over at the prince before continuing.

"Duke Ferdinand," he said.

"What!" the king said.

"Tell us your name and rank," Arkády commanded.

The soldier motioned for more wine.

"Sir Eumen von Lettów," he said. "I was assigned as a military adviser and trainer to the Duke of Mährenia's army. We started from Rautenstahl, heading down the Cacÿparis River into Pommerelia. We invested Trüdigar, and captured it on the ninth, with almost no casualties. Three days later at Kölkeimás we 'whelmed Count Theodebert's army, and then attacked the citadel itself. The castle fell on the seventeenth."

He sipped more wine, swallowing heavily, and wiped his hand on his dirty breeches, before continuing.

"We followed the Kleine due east from Kölkeimás, meeting only partisans, figuring either to strike out from the river when it turned south, or to run with it straight into the Ærénosë, and then march along that waterway to Balíxira. Tuesday night we camped along the river bank, posting most of our scouts and pickets to the east. I was sent north into Martandö to ride my customary circuit.

"I had stopped to answer a call of nature when I heard some riders coming fast just to the south of me. I quickly blindfolded and tethered my mount, and climbed partway up a tree. A large mounted force of Pommerelians, four or five thousand at least, was moving through the night. I followed at a distance, hoping somehow to find a way through to the other side to warn our men.

"Then I heard the attack. Most of our boys were caught unawares. They were slaughtered in their beds. I could see hundreds of tents burning in the wind, and the unarmed men highlighted against them as they were run down by enemy troops. Some tried to escape in the river, and were swept away. Some were captured, I don't know how many. Others fled. I don't know what became of Duke Ferdinand. But the army of Mährenia is utterly destroyed as an effective fighting force, of that I'm sure.

"So I rode east into the night, wanting to warn you, stopping only to steal a horse when the one I was riding threatened to drop."

Prince Arkády took the lead in questioning.

"Sir Eumen," he said, "you stated that you saw Duke Ferdinand's army being attacked, but you also indicated that you were watching the battle from a distance."

"Yes, Highness," the soldier said.

"How much of a distance?" the prince asked.

"Maybe a mile," Eumen acknowledged.

"Maybe more?" Arkády prodded.

The scout slowly nodded his head.

"Then how can you really know what happened?" Arkády said. "You've admitted that you didn't see the duke taken, and you obviously don't know whether or not the Mährenians were able to regroup. All you *can* say for sure is that there was a Pommerelian raid on the camp during the early morning hours. Why didn't you spot the enemy forces sooner?"

"I, well...," the soldier stammered out.

"You were asleep, weren't you?" Arkády said.

Eumen let his head drop.

"Yes, sir," he finally said.

"Then tell me again what you *do* know," the prince said.

The soldier gulped audibly.

"Well, sir, I had dozed off against a tree, when my horse snorted. I looked out from the grove and saw a large troop marching by, I don't know how many. It was just too dark to see. I followed them at a great distance to avoid being detected, and heard them attack our camp. I did see some fires among the tents and noted a few men outlined against them who were cut down, but I don't know how many. I fled the scene as quickly as possible, knowing I would be blamed."

"Very well," Arkády said. "Sire?"

The king grimaced at the task before him.

"Sir Eumen von Lettów," he said, "you are charged by us with malfeasance of duty and cowardice in the face of battle. How plead you?"

"Guilty, majesty," the soldier said.

"Then it is the judgment of this court," Kipriyán said, "that you be stripped of your titles, estates, and family name, and at the first light of morning, be taken to a place of execution, there to receive the ultimate punishment. But because you have made an effort to warn us of the dangers that we face, and because you have freely admitted your guilt to this court and council, we grant you the merciful kiss of the axe."

Eumen bowed deeply, and touched his head to the table.

"I accept your judgment, Sire, and humbly beg your forgiveness."

"It is given," the king said.

Then he motioned to the guards.

"Take him away."

The War Council spent the next two hours discussing their options.

"If Ferdinand *is* dead," Arkády said, "then we must act very quickly to have Prince Nikolaí declared king. We can't allow Duchess Johanna to seize control of the government by proclaiming herself Regent for an underaged Princess Rosanna."

"And if he *isn't?*" Nikolaí asked.

Arkády smiled.

"Then we might offend him most mightily, my dear royal brother," he said.

"I don't want anyone to forget my second son," Humfried said, "or *his* rights. If you proclaim Nikolaí King of Mährenia, then you must also declare Prince Norbert the new Duke of Nisyria."

King Kipriyán shook his head in frustration.

"We will not forget, *Cousin*," he said. "Gad, how *could* we?"

Lord Gorázd waved his hand to get the king's attention.

"I think it would be wise, majesty," he said, "to assume the worst, and to proceed with the official proclamations tomorrow. We have no way of confirming what exactly happened on the Kleine, but that a battle occurred there is now apparent. If Duke Ferdinand is dead or wounded, then clearly Prince Nikolaí is his lawful successor under the terms of our treaty. If our proclamation proves premature, we can apologize and step back a few paces. But not to proceed immediately might well leave a vacuum that someone less suitable could fill."

There was general support from around the table for this course of action.

The king stated: "Very well, my lords. Tomorrow at *tritê* we will declare my second son King of Mährenia and Duke of Dürkheim, and Prince Humfried's second son will be named Duke of Nisyria and Count of Cartágö. Agreed?"

Without dissension, all concurred, and the meeting was adjourned.

CHAPTER TWENTY-TWO
"A FEW COUNTERS ON A BOARD"

"*Please*, Tréssa."

Queen Polyxena was seated with her sister-in-law in a secluded corner of the bright, airy solar at Tighrishály Palace in Paltyrrha.

"You *must* eat something," she said.

She held a tempting spoonful of rich broth to Princess Teréza's pale lips.

The princess tried to smile at her brother's wife, but it came out all wrong. The crooked grimace that slashed across her wan face was ghastly.

"I'm just not hungry, Xena." Teréza shuddered. "I *think* I am, and then when I sit down and actually try a bite or two, my appetite suddenly goes away. It's been like that ever since poor Dolph was killed earlier this year...." She stifled a sob.

"I know, dearest, and I understand."

The queen reached over and tenderly brushed a lock of drifting hair away from her sister-in-law's pinched face.

"But you must try," Polyxena said. "You must center yourself and really try this time, for Ezzö's sake as well as your own."

"...And I had the strangest feeling, at Körösladány a few weeks ago...," Tréssa rambled on, as if the queen had not spoken, "...that I'd never see my Ezzösh again. He shouldn't have gone, Xena."

She gripped the other woman's hand with her little claw.

"He wouldn't listen to me, so I sent Élla to talk to him, but he just kept saying that he had to go, that it was his duty."

Teréza looked around the lovely room, but saw nothing pleasant there.

"He's not well, you know," she went on. "For the last year or so, he's been forgetting things. Little things at first. One moment he'll seem perfectly fine, and then he won't remember an appointment he made a week ago, even though I've reminded him of it several times. He's been worse lately. His great-grand-papá went the same way, I'm told."

She got up and began pacing the floor as she spoke.

"I begged him not to go," she said. "I got down on my hands and knees, Xena, and begged him. But he said he'd rather die in battle, if his time has come, than to linger like the old Humfried, not even knowing who he was. Oh dear sister," she sobbed, flinging herself at Polyxena's feet.

"Tell me true, I must know," Teréza said. "Is there any news at all from the front?"

The queen's face was grim as she helped Teréza back to her chair.

"Things are not all that bad," the queen said. "You know that Ezzö and Pankratz have taken Lockenlöd Castle in Einwegflasche, killing Count Iselin in the process. That's good news, surely!"

However, Polyxena also knew that Iselin's son and heir, Lord Kortis, had escaped with a group of his men, but she did not mention that fact to Teréza.

"Humfried and Kipriyán are still besieging Karkára in southern Einwegflasche, I'm told," the queen said. "There's been no word at all from Duke Ferdinand's army, except that 'they're somewhere' out in that godforsaken plain they call the Prüffenmark. 'So far, so good,' as they say. Everyone seems satisfied with the progress we've made with 'a minimum of casualties'."

"Then why do I sense you're worried, too?" The princess stared deep into Polyxena's eyes.

"Because, my dearest," the queen said, increasing her

defenses just a bit, "I care about them as much as you do. I hate this war and what it's doing to us. There are no certainties in battle. A great triumph one day can become a greater tragedy the next."

Once again she offered a spoonful of broth, and this time, soothed by Polyxena's voice, Teréza accepted it, swallowing with some effort, but keeping it down.

"Even if you 'win'," the queen said, "someone you love can be killed or maimed in the process. Our men never think of their families waiting for them back home. To them it's all such a grand adventure. And when it's all done with, why, then they can spin yarns about it around the bonfire. They can tell war stories to their grandchildren in their old age."

She kept spooning the broth into Teréza's mouth as she spoke, like a mother bird feeding her chick.

"They never think of their women waiting, always waiting, growing old wondering if they'll ever return in one piece," she said. "Oh, yes! They call us 'foolish' for worrying about them. They march off to battle, still believing in happy endings, the poor fools. They think that by moving a few counters on a board, they will prevail, as if any of that really mattered. Whatever happiness we find in our lifetime, Tréssa, is paid for with our suffering. Only women understand *that* little secret. So that is why you must eat, sister. *You* must still be here, strong and smiling, when your hunter finally comes home from the hill."

Teréza grimaced. "And if he *doesn't* come home? What do I do then? I'm not strong like you, Xena. Sometimes I feel as if I've already experienced all the sorrows a person should be made to bear in a lifetime. Five children, Xena, *five children.* First it was little Emíliya, dead of the spotted pox. She was only five. Then came my other girl, Triféna, struck down by paralysis at age eleven. Then poor Kóstya was killed in that stupid duel. Then this thing with Dolph. Now only Humfried is left, and he's cruel and unfeeling. Oh yes, I know my son's faults better than anyone. I know what the people think of him. But he's still my son, sister, my *only* surviving son. If he and Ezzösh don't return,

I don't know if I can bear it, I just don't know anymore...."

"Then let us do the only thing left to us. Pray with me, Tréssa," Xena said, "pray with me for the safe return of our loved ones. Let us pray most earnestly, for their salvation and for our own."

The two women clasped hands and bowed their heads, one dark and one light, to pray to their Lord Jesus Christ. Their urgent whispers rose up like sweet-smelling incense, and commingled with the myriad tiny twinkling motes floating aimlessly in the sunlight. They stayed there for some time, beseeching their God to send their brave, foolish men home safe to them.

CHAPTER TWENTY-THREE
"A LOST SOUL"

Elsewhere in Tighrishály Palace, the governess Márissa had summoned the Princesses Dúra and Arrhiána to the nursery to comfort little Rÿna, who had awakened screaming from her afternoon nap.

"Mamá, Mamá!" the child called out in terror.

"What *is* it, Rÿna?" her mother said, gently shaking her awake. "What on earth is the matter with you?"

"*I saw him!*" The little girl panted, clinging for dear life to her mother's hand.

"*Whom* did you see?" Arrhiána knelt on the other side of the princess's canopied bed, and reached across to stroke her niece's perspiring brow. "What are you talking about, dearest?"

"The Da-Dark-Haired Ma-Man!" Rÿna said.

Crystalline tears etched a bright path down her perfect, heart-shaped face.

"Try to tell us exactly what you saw," said Arrhiána, probing the child gently with her mind, finding the beginnings of defenses, but nothing sophisticated. Then she siphoned away some of Rÿna's fear.

"He was big and hairy," the girl began, calmer now, "and he was chasing poor Grandpapá 'round and 'round the council table, and Grandpapá was huffing and puffing and going slower and slower, and the Dark-Haired Man was getting closer to him, and I was afraid, so I screamed, and then the Dark-Haired Man stopped and *looked right at me!*, and *I* wet myself."

She stopped, pink with embarrassment.

"Oh, Mamá, I'm so sorry." She started to cry again.

"Listen to me, little one," Dúra said. "It's all right. Don't worry about the bedclothes. I don't mind. It's easily taken care of...."

Dúra crooned to her daughter, rocking the child back and forth on her shoulder. She looked past her to Arrhiána and shook her head.

Arrhiána tried another tack.

"Rÿna, look at me," she said. "*Rÿna!*"

The girl slowly turned her face towards her aunt, who continued speaking quietly.

"There *is* no Dark-Haired Man," Arrhiána said. "It's a story, that's all, something that one of the bards or troubadours made up while sitting around a campfire so that people would give him food or shelter. He doesn't exist, any more than hobgoblins exist. They're just fanciful tales."

Rÿna canted her head like a bird.

"Oh, no, Auntie Rhie," she said in her little singsong voice, "you're wrong! He *is* real. I *know* he is."

Arrhiána was perplexed at the child's certainty.

"*How* do you know, dearest?"

"Ouisa told me," the little girl said, on more familiar ground now, "and she never lies."

"But Ouisa's just your doll, isn't she?" her aunt said. "She's not alive, not like we're alive. She can't really talk to you."

"*Oh, yes, she can!*" Rÿna said. "We talk all the time, 'bout lots of things. She's a, a lost soul or something like that. That's what she says, anyway."

"'A lost soul,' is she?" Rhie snorted. "Well, bring her to me. Let's just see how well she talks to me!"

"I don't know, Auntie," the girl said. "She never talks to anybody else. But I'll go get her and see."

Rÿna climbed down off her bed and ran over to the corner of the room, where her toys were arranged in a tall cabinet stenciled with fanciful designs. She rummaged around until she found her favorite rag doll, and carried it back to her aunt.

"You won't hurt her, will you?" she asked, handing over her prized possession.

"No, Rÿna. I promise I won't hurt her," Arrhiána said.

Rhie turned the doll over, and carefully examined it from every angle, moving its jointed limbs back and forth, and removing its well-worn clothing to reveal a stuffed cloth body. But she could discover nothing unusual about the toy. She tried a mental probe, but sensed only emptiness. *No!* There was something more, almost a bleakness, a quality less than nothingness. Suddenly the doll twisted in her hands.

"Ouch!" she said, pulling her right hand away.

On her palm was a spot of blood. Arrhiána turned Ouisa over and felt very carefully along its spine.

"What is it, Rhie?" Dúra asked, clearly concerned.

"Ah," her sister-in-law said. "Here it is. Just a needle poking through the fabric."

"A needle!" Dúra drew nearer to see. "What in the world is *that* doing there?"

Arrhiána carefully extracted a shiny metal sliver about an inch long from the stuffed body.

"Wicked little thing, isn't it? It's good that I found it. You could have been hurt, Rÿna."

"Ouisa would never hurt *me*, Auntie," the child said, "only...."

She paused a beat, as if debating the wisdom of what she was about to say.

"Only what?" Arrhiána said. "Speak up, child!"

"Ouisa would only hurt someone else if they were trying to hurt *me*." Rÿna drew herself up imperiously. "She said no one can hurt me ever again. She promised I won't be lonely ever again."

"Dearest!" Arrhiána said.

She stooped down to the child's level, so she was looking straight into Rÿna's blue eyes.

"There are worse things than being lonely. There are worse things than feeling pain. Someday you'll understand, I hope.

You have a mother and a father who adore you more than anything in the world. And I love you too. You're the best little girl I know."

She gave her a comforting squeeze.

"Now, please tell Ouisa she's not to go about hurting people," Rhie said, "that's not a very nice thing to do. I think it's time you forgot all of this, and went outside to play in the garden."

Arrhiána gave her a mental nudge, blurring her memory of the nightmare.

"There, that's a good girl," she said, as her niece went scampering off with Ouisa, chattering away to the doll.

"Thanks for your help, Rhie. You have a real way with her," Dúra said, shaking her head. "Sometimes I can't help wondering if she was left on my pillow by the fairies. She's so smart, it frightens me. I wasn't at all like that at her age."

"Well...." Arrhiána laughed, "I have to tell you that she's a *lot* like me, when I was young. Kásha, too, if you want the truth. I'm afraid she just inherited that Tighrishi bloody-mindedness that you see so often in our line. You didn't know what you were getting into when you married Kásha, did you?"

"I didn't have much choice, did I? Not when your father and my father sat down together at the bargaining table!"

Dúra smiled at her sister-in-law.

"I have to admit, though," she said, "that marrying Kásha was the *best* thing that could have happened to me. I couldn't have chosen a better husband for myself. He's strong-minded, all right, I admit that, but he's also kind and gentle, and oh so handsome! My heart still skips a beat whenever he enters the room. Oh, yes, it does!" she continued, when Arrhiána made a disgusted face at her.

She reached out on impulse and patted Arrhiána's hand.

"I just wish we could send a little bit of our happiness your way, Rhie. My prayer is that you could find someone one day who would give you even half of what Kásha gives me."

"I'm perfectly content as I am, Drúsha," Arrhiána said. "I'm really not turning over the stones, hoping to find a suitable prince lurking under one of them. I'd be more likely to uncover a toad!" She chortled. "If it happens, it happens, and you'll be the first to know, I promise. Right now, there are other things I want to do with my life."

"Other things? *What* other things?" Dúra asked.

Arrhiána brushed her fair hair back from her face.

"I was thinking of writing a book about the family, *our* family, I mean. It's such a fascinating group of people, really, and no one has ever written a history focused entirely on the Tighrishi. Oh, there've been chronicles aplenty published, and the usual, very dull, over-embellished accounts of this king or that, or this war or that. But no one's ever done what I have in mind. Something honest."

"Honest!" Dúra laughed out loud at the suggestion. "Your Papá would never let the ink dry on a page before tearing it all to shreds. Besides, who would read such a thing? People want romance, not reality. They want to escape their cares, not listen to someone else's troubles."

"Oh, I think there'd be a lot of people who'd pay the scribes for copies of what I have in mind." Arrhiána joined her sister-in-law with a chuckle of her own. "Although, I dare say, it might be for reasons other than they usually buy such things. This book might actually get read!"

Outside, they could hear Rÿna playing happily with her dolls in the Hanging Garden, her tinkling laughter bubbling up like Mösza's old fountain in Land's End.

"She's such a good little soul," Arrhiána said. "I do hope she...." But she stopped herself, leaving unspoken what was really on her mind.

"Come, Dúra," she continued, offering her arm, "it's time we went to see how Mamá is doing with poor Aunt Tréssa."

CHAPTER TWENTY-FOUR
"IT'S THE DARK-HAIRED MAN!"

That evening, King Kipriyán prepared for bed as usual, rubbing his teeth with a solution of horsepiss to keep them white, and then rinsing his mouth out with wine.

"Gad, that stuff tastes awful," he said to his servant, Siméon. "Be glad you're not a king, Sim."

"Yes, majesty," said his aide. "Is there anything else you wish for this evening?"

"No, that's quite enough for one day, I think." The old man sighed. "I wonder where Ferdinand is tonight."

He pulled on a simple white nightshift trimmed in purple.

"You may leave," he said.

He knelt on the bare ground next to his bed, and said a prayer to Almighty God, begging for His forgiveness and for His support of their enterprise, and also praying for the soul of Duke Ferdinand, if he were really dead. Finally, he asked God to vanquish the Dark-Haired Man. *Amen*, he finished, and crossed himself.

Then he pulled back his cover, and screamed, long and loud.

Within a moment his tent was crowded with guards, sons, courtiers, and metropolitans.

"What is it, sire?" Arkády asked.

"L-look," the king said, stammering, and then pointed at the bed.

There, where his head would have lain, was a six-inch lock of dark, shaggy hair, like the leavings of some savage beast. The prince picked it up, and rolled it between his fingers.

"I don't know what this is," he finally said, passing it around to the others.

But no one could identify the animal from which it had come.

"It's the Dark-Haired Man!" the king cried.

They all looked back and forth amongst each other, afraid that he might be right.

"Majesty!"

Bishop Varlaám was standing just beyond the princes.

"This is the Devil's work. You should be exorcised."

The old patriarch, who was roused from his bed, wearily and reluctantly agreed. Exorcisms, once begun, had a way of leading to other things much less palatable. Varlaám was delegated to perform the ceremony. The king consented to have all of the leading men of the court, all of the royal family, and all of the generals, also included.

Varlaám made them wait for two full hours while he gathered together the necessary implements and special prayer-books. The ceremony itself took another three hours, so that, by the time they all had been cleansed of Satan's pernicious influence, they had also lost much of their night's sleep.

The king was in a foul mood by the time he finally got back to bed. He spent the rest of the night tossing back and forth under the covers, being chased through his dreams by the Dark-Haired Man. Only once did he sleep undisturbed, when his granddaughter Rÿna somehow distracted the beast's attention.

CHAPTER TWENTY-FIVE
"YOUR WAR IS OVER"

Three days later, on the Feast of Saint Genesios, Prince Kiríll led a force of five hundred men up the canyon of the River Vá'al to attack the walled city of Karkára high in the Carpates Mountains. At the same time, Prince Nikolaí moved five thousand Kórynthi soldiers into position before the main gate of the citadel to take advantage of any diversion or opening that Kiríll might be able to create.

Kiríll's men traveled half the distance through the gorge during the afternoon, then stopped to rest. They started again just after sundown, using the light of the near full moon that was coming up over the horizon to show them the way. The prince had ordered them to fashion makeshift, single-strut ladders in sections that could be broken down and then retied together at will; these had been strapped to their backs, causing several of the riders to lose their seats when the protruding pieces caught on bushes along the narrow trail. One man toppled into the gorge with his mount, dutifully choosing not to scream as he fell to certain death.

As the stream began to peter out, Kiríll finally called a halt to their procession, ordering them to dismount and proceed the rest of the way on foot.

"Çévik," he called to his scout, "what's up ahead?"

The man pointed to the ridge above them.

"Just beyond the heights," he whispered, "is the Valley of the Gáll. Karkára lies about three miles southwest, near a small lake called Örr. The main road runs right through the city, but we'll be coming out on the north side. Although the north wall is relatively open, it's inaccessible except by this back route, unless you cross the lake by boat, or climb a sheer rock face on the other side. They won't be expecting us."

"Very good." The prince turned to his chief officer. "Commander Willibald, let's proceed," he said.

And so they started up the winding trail, which crossed back and forth several times before they reached the top. Then they proceeded quietly until they approached the last cove of trees before the open field in front of the north wall of Karkára Castle.

"Can you see any of the guards?" Kiríll whispered.

Çévik silently motioned to several points along the twenty-foot-high stone walls, where the prince could pick out a half dozen enemy soldiers dutifully marching up and down the palisades, watching the empty ground below them. The moon lit up the field as brightly as if a ball had been scheduled there.

"Damn!" Kiríll muttered to himself.

To Willibald, he whispered: "Quietly begin assembling the ladders. When that's finished, order the men to rest."

They would have to wait for the moon to set to have any realistic chance of penetrating the citadel.

Around them the men unpacked their burdens. Each "ladder" consisted of a single piece of wood crosshatched with wooden slats. One end of the piece was beveled, and the other incut to match. In theory, the various ladders could be lashed together to form a structure stable enough to get an army over the walls of Karkára. In practice, some of the sections wouldn't fit together no matter what they did, and were discarded, while others, although they fit, wouldn't remain stable. In the end, they had just seven workable ladders.

A few hours before dawn, the moon finally slipped behind the protruding peaks looming all around them, and the assault was ready to begin. Prince Kiríll ordered Willibald to prepare for the attack. In the blackness following moonset, they hoped at least to reach the wall before they were detected by the watchers above.

As quickly and quietly as possible, they ran the few hundred yards across the open field. One man tripped over a root, and fell with a jangle. Above them, they heard one of the guards ask another, "What's that!" Then the ladders were going up, and five hundred men were climbing them hand over hand as fast as they could go.

Kiríll and Çévik were the first over the wall, and immediately encountered two of the enemy right in front of them. Instinctively, the prince parried the blow directed at him, and ran the soldier through with his own sword. Then began a flurry of blow and counterblow, as the Kórynthi force poured over the battlements in a wave of flashing weapons.

The half dozen Pommerelian guards were swept away immediately, without an alarum being given. Kiríll and his men were already heading around the palisades toward the guardhouse controlling the main gate before anyone there knew they had been invaded. Suddenly, there was a shout down below, and a clanging as the sergeants began rousting their men. Still, no one managed to reinforce the battlements before Kiríll reached the gate.

A desperate battle was fought there between the fifteen Pommerelians in the control house, and the twenty or thirty Kórynthi soldiers immediately trailing the prince. Kiríll took a blow to his head that left the world swimming, but continued to push forward. His left arm was red with blood from his shoulder down. Then the Pommerelian guards were dead, all of them!

Kiríll ordered Çévik to help him, and placed the others behind them to ward off the expected attackers. Together with the scout, and using his right arm only, he began to turn the great wheel that wound the cable that lifted the main gate. Slowly they winched it up, and as soon as it had reached the two-foot level, Kórynthi soldiers from Nikolaí's brigade began sliding under it, and wedging huge pieces of wood around the bottom sides to keep it from accidentally releasing on top of them. Now it was going faster, and the press of troops into the city became a flood.

Karkára officially fell an hour later, when Pommerelian General Conradin was killed defending the central citadel. The rest of his men promptly laid down their arms and surrendered.

King Kipriyán found his son still propped against the wall of the control house, being treated by a physician.

"How bad is it?" he asked, fearing the worst.

"He'll live," was the response from Fra Tibor. "I don't know how soon he'll be able to use his left arm again, but unless it festers, he'll survive to sire a dozen grandsons. I've done all I can do for the moment," he said, turning to another wounded man nearby.

Kipriyán gazed upon his third son with pride.

"You've done well, my boy," he said. "I wish I'd been there myself."

"Thank you, father." Kiríll's voice was weak. "Would you give me a hand, please."

"Of course," said the king, happy to assist. "You've earned your rest, Kir. Your war is over."

CHAPTER TWENTY-SIX
"NOW *THAT'S* A DAINTY TREAT!"

A week later, on the Feast of Saint Barnabas the Beggar of Barstö, the two halves of the Kórynthi military pincers finally met at Saint Paulinos's Abbey on the southern Töklos Plain. King Kipriyán's force had slowly wheeled north around the protruding point of the Läuterung Hills, while the Bolémi soldiers of the Princes Ezzö and Pankratz had marched south by southwest through the very heart of Einwegflasche, meeting only scattered opposition. Their combined forces were now poised to strike a deathblow directly into the heartland of Pommerelia.

Kipriyán's men had arrived first on the previous day. Thus, that monarch was standing with King Humfried in front of the monastery gates when the first units of the northern army appeared.

"All hail to the Kings of Pommerelia and Kórynthia," Prince Ezzö said, bowing his head.

He seemed more himself than he had in months.

"We greet the conquerors of Lockenlöd Castle," Kipriyán returned.

Prince Pankratz reached into his saddlebag, pulling out a leather sack.

"We bring you a present, *Cousin*," he said, "a rare boor from the north country."

He shook the container upside down, and out popped the grisly, blood-stained head of Iselin late Count of Einwegflasche.

It bounced once on the dusty ground before coming to rest on its side. The empty eye sockets were crawling with maggots.

King Kipriyán laughed.

"Now *that's* a dainty treat," he joked.

"Siméon," he ordered his aide, "put it on a pike and anchor it to the gate, *here*," pointing out the exact spot where he wanted it placed for best viewing.

"Humphy!" came a yell, as Queen Pulkhériya stepped out of her carriage, the Princesses Minérva and Salentína trailing behind.

"Cherie?" King Humfried said. "What in blazes are *you* doing here?"

"Oh," she said, "we just had to come and see your great victory over the Walküri."

"Daddy!" came the second call, as little Salentína rushed over and hugged her father.

"Tína?" Then, glaring at his son: "Pánky, can I see you for a moment?"

Humfried briefly ignored his wife and daughter and dragged his heir to one side.

"What *is* this?" he asked. "You know better than to bring these women into a war zone. Whatever possessed you, son?"

"Father, they insisted on coming," Prince Pankratz said. "What could I do?"

"You *could* have said 'no'," the king said. "Now, we're stuck with the ladies, and I'm going to have to detail a company of men just to guard them. I'll have to see if I can persuade them to transit back home. I'm greatly disappointed, Pankratz."

"I'm truly sorry, father," the prince said, hanging his head. "I can see now that I made a poor decision. I'll try to do better."

"Enough said," Humfried replied. "Still, it's good to see you, lad. I hear you've done well up north. How's father?"

"He seems somewhat better," Pankratz said. "I think being where he can do something physical has helped him quite a bit. And he's more cheerful than I've seen him in the last year."

"So he seems," the king said. "Well, we'd better get back to the women, or they'll be the next ones declaring war!"

They both chuckled at the idea.

After celebrating the unification of their forces with a dinner that evening in the abbey house, the two kings called a joint meeting of the War Council, to discuss strategies for the final phase of the conflict.

As usual, it was Prince Arkády who made the initial presentation.

"Highnesses," he said, "the combined Kórynthi army now consists of approximately thirty thousand cavalry, infantry, and support troops, organized into four corps under the leadership of Prince Pankratz, Prince Nikolaí, Prince Zakháry, and myself. We are being supplied by three separate trains of wagons coming through the Kultúra, Skopélosz, and Karkára Passes, as well as from local sources that we've managed to scavenge ourselves. Although our supply lines have been attacked by partisans, as expected, we have managed to get regular shipments through in sufficient quantities to feed our men.

"We have confirmed," he said, "that Duke Ferdinand is missing and his army destroyed"—there were groans from around the table—"and that Prince Walther's force survived the battle largely untouched. Our scouts report that the prince has returned to Balíxira. He and his men have rejoined his father's main army."

"How many men do they have?" Prince Nikolaí asked.

"Sir Léka estimates somewhere around seventeen to twenty thousand soldiers," his brother said. "The number is difficult to assess, because their corps operate semi-independently from each other, and because the irregular forces that provide an adjunct to the Pommerelian army often fade in and out of the Läuterung Highlands."

"Can we count on the Arrhénis for any additional help?" Humfried asked.

"Probably not." Arkády sighed. "The last word we had, yesterday, is that Count Sándor's men were just approaching Myláßgorod. They'll need to rest for at least a day or two before assaying the pass. The Skopélosz Road is packed with wagons, soldiers, messengers, and wounded coming and going, making transit very slow. Realistically, they won't get here in time to make any difference."

"What's the terrain like between Saint Paulinos and Balíxira?" Prince Kiríll said.

His left arm was bound in a sling and healing nicely, but he had been relieved of command until he was completely well again.

Prince Arkády turned to face his brother.

"Léka tells me that it's mostly rolling green hills," he said, "if we stay west of the Läuterungs, which are more treacherous and full of rugged canyons. All we need to do is follow the Falling Water River south until we hit Balíxira."

Nikolaí raised his hand again.

"Is there any place where the Pommerelians can gain some material advantage?" he asked.

Arkády shook his head.

"Not if we stay out of the highlands," he said. "In my estimation, they'll have to try stopping us before we reach Balíxira. They just can't afford to lose their oldest and most prestigious city."

"How far away is their main army?" Nikolaí asked.

"Léka says two or three days at most. Of course, they could very easily move closer or further away as we march towards them.

"Now," he continued, "we do have a number of small problems that need to be addressed immediately. The joining of the armies has created some temporary shortages of beef, feed, and medications. King Humfried's men are tired from marching across the great plain, and both of our forces need to be integrated smoothly under one command. Therefore, I suggest that we wait here a day or two before proceeding south."

"I disagree," Nikolaí said. "As I've said before, the quicker that we move, the less prepared the enemy will be."

Each of the council members spoke in turn, dividing about

equally on the question. Finally, Kipriyán spoke.

"We will rest one day," he ordered, "and begin marching again on the day after tomorrow."

"I suggest, sire," Arkády said, "that we continue posting our scouts as widely through the surrounding countryside as possible, to avoid getting pulled into a trap."

"An excellent idea," the king said. "Any further questions?"

"Arkásha, just what do you know about this, uh, Falling River?" Nikolaí asked.

"The Falling Water begins somewhat north of here on the Töklos Plain," his brother said, "erupting right out of the ground from a large spring. South of Saint Paulinos, the river starts cutting a valley through the hills, just skirting the western part of the Läuterungs. After picking up a number of creeks coming out of the highlands, the watercourse deepens considerably and the river quickly becomes impassable. If we stay to the right of the gorge, we should have a clear road all the way to Balíxira, and we'll be well protected on our left flank."

"Are we agreed?" King Kipriyán asked, looking around at each council member. They all nodded, one by one. "Very well, then. *For God and Kórynthia!*" he shouted.

"*For God and Kórynthia!*" came the unanimous response.

CHAPTER TWENTY-SEVEN
"WHY DO YOU CALL
ME DAUGHTER?"

In Paltyrrha on that same day the Princess Arrhiána, Regent of the Kingdom of Kórynthia, asked Metropolitan Timotheos, *Locum Tenens* of the Holy Church, to conduct a prayer service for the success of the expedition in Pommerelia, and for the safe return of the soldiers and their officers.

Earlier that morning, she had transited to Kórynthály, and sought out her sister, Princess Sachette, to return her to court. When the Lady Dómnina, Abbess of Saint Exouperantia's Convent, objected, Arrhiána overruled her, saying that the war had created hardships and demands on everyone, and that God would surely understand why she needed to borrow one of His chosen ones for a few months.

"Oh, Rhie, I'm so excited!" Sachette said, almost babbling in her excitement. "I haven't been to Paltyrrha in years and years. What's it like now?"

Arrhiána just laughed.

"Overcrowded, dirty, chaotic, hectic," she said. "And exciting, energizing, and full of life."

"I can't wait," her sister said.

And so, when Timotheos began his service later that afternoon, the two sisters stood together in the front rank of Saint Konstantín's Cathedral, representing the Royal House of Tighris before the multitude of celebrants. Arrhiána allowed her sibling to touch her hand throughout the ceremony, so that Chette could see the great icons and stained glass windows through her elder sister's eyes.

Oooh! Sachette exclaimed mentally. *Such beautiful colors!*

Lovely, aren't they? Arrhiána agreed. *See Saint Konstantín and Saint Yeléna over on the right. And Saint Apollináry the Apologist, Saint Plautílla the Martyr, Saint Ksanfíppa, Saint Tíkhon, and oh so many others.*

But no Saint Sachette, her sister said.

You'll be the first, my love, Arrhiána indicated.

Sachette blushed. *I'm not good enough to be a saint.*

I think you're the best of all of us, her older sister said.

What's that? Sachette asked, pointing mentally to a shadowy alcove on the left that housed a side altar.

Where? Arrhiána inquired, looking around, but unable to penetrate the dark with her eyes.

The metropolitan droned on with his service.

There! I can feel someone over near the altar, the girl continued. *He's saying something to me about the war, that Papá must turn back before all is lost. I don't understand, Rhie. Now, he says that magic started this war, and magic will end it. He says the Tighrishi are to blame for all the killing and the terror, that what we do to our own is what we feel compelled to do to others. He says we have warped what we were given. He says we have to change.*

I don't see anyone! Arrhiána said.

"Guard," she called quietly to one side.

"Yes, Highness," said the nearest soldier.

"Please check that small altar on the left and see if there's anyone hiding there," Arrhiána ordered.

"At once, Highness," he said, and headed off into the alcove.

He returned a moment later, shaking his head. "Nothing, Highness," he mouthed silently.

"Thank you, Gilár," she softly replied.

Then, mentally to Sachette: *Is he still there?*

Oh, yes, the girl stated. *He's praying with us.*

Who is he? Arrhiána asked, trying to contain her terror.

He's one of us, Sachette said, *I'm sure of it. He's...*

But Arrhiána could wait no longer, and surged into her sister's mind without waiting for permission, forging a link with the presence that she too could now sense hovering in the shadows.

Who are *you?* she asked. *Why do you threaten us?*

Arrhiána suddenly was filled with a sense of great wisdom and sadness and compassion, as the being gently connected with her mind.

Are you...He? she asked.

Oh, no, daughter, hardly that, came the reply. *Not even a saint.* She had a feeling of loving humor envelop her. *Just a humble servant of the Almighty.*

Then why *do you call me daughter?* Arrhiána asked.

When you can find the answer to that question in your heart, dear Arrhiánakicsi, the presence whispered, *then come and see me, and we will talk again. Now, I must go. Do not despair, my daughter, even when the darkness seems to 'whelm you. Good will yet prevail.*

Then he was gone from their minds, just like that, and they both felt an immense sense of longing for his presence.

In front of the altar, the Metropolitan Timotheos finished the last of his prayers.

"Amen," he chanted.

"Amen," the two women replied.

CHAPTER TWENTY-EIGHT

"BRUGA!"

In Neustria, the time of birthing had come at last. The Princess Brislaine, at full term, had begun her contractions some eight hours earlier. Cheerfully, she had announced this fact to her ladies-in-waiting, adding, "Well, if it's no worse than this, I just don't know what all the fuss is about!"

Adèle had merely raised her eyes ceilingward, chuckling inwardly at her daughter's *naïveté*. She then set about notifying Mirza and the royals, and making the necessary household arrangements.

The princess was soon ensconced in the large comfortable suite in the royal palace set aside for this purpose. She sat propped up in bed, gaily ordering people about, determined to make the most of her moment of glory. Her ladies and their maids scurried to and fro, making sure that the linens were fresh, the water scalded, and that all was prepared for the great event.

The female members of the royal family set themselves up in shifts, taking turns all day long. They walked back and forth with their young charge, catering to her whims, encouraging her and keeping her calm.

Later in the day, as the dull aching sensation in her lower back became more pronounced, she began to understand just what "all the fuss" was about. She moved inexorably toward the final phase of the struggle which would bring forth her firstborn son into the world.

"Push!" the midwife Mirza was demanding. "Is close, now. Push it you must right out of zere, child," she added with a sinister smirk, "or it vill stay inside you and fester."

"I'm *trying* to push!" Laine gasped in frustration, tears filling her lovely eyes. "Granny, where are you?" she cried out, as yet another spasm rolled over her.

"I'm right here, love." Brisquayne shoved Mirza aside, glaring angrily at her. She had insisted on staying in the room from the very beginning, refusing all other offers to spell her. She had been watching Mirza carefully. Now she was prepared to interfere with the proceedings, if she deemed it necessary.

"Hold on to me and relax just a moment," she whispered. "Ignore her. You should wait until the next pain comes before you try pushing again. Let me know and I'll help you."

She wrapped one of her granddaughter's hands in her own, touching rings and pouring her strength through the quickly-established link.

Laine's contractions were harder and lasting longer now, and the dowager queen knew from years of experience that the final stage of labor was close at hand.

Suddenly she became aware of a subtle change taking place, deep within her granddaughter's body. Something was delaying the force of nature! She looked up and caught Mirza smiling down at her triumphantly.

"*Bruga!*" she breathed, and surged angrily through the link into her granddaughter's form and mind, striking out at all the foreign interference that was threatening the birth.

Mirza was caught off guard, and almost lost contact. Then she fought back even more savagely. Laine nearly lost consciousness, but on some primitive level of her being, the mothering instinct asserted itself. She knew something was terribly wrong now, and she gamely held on, aligning her own waning strength with that of her grandmother. Together they began the struggle to save her child and herself.

The next half hour was a nightmare, as the two older women pushed and pulled around and through Laine's pale form. Small advantages were gained and lost, and wars were waged unto the bitterest of ends. No one else in the room seemed aware of the desperate battle being fought right there in front of them.

Brisquayne was on the verge of exhaustion when she remembered something she had forgotten about, something from her distant past. It just might work! She flashed a mental picture of someone else she had once known at court, someone Mösza had known, too.

The midwife suddenly reeled back as if she had been struck. Abruptly, her rings flaring, she broke off all physical and psychic contact with both Laine and her grandmother.

"I, I don't feel vell," Mirza muttered. "Must get air," she added, rushing from the room.

"Well, I'll be...!" Adèle looked after the woman, shaking her head. Glancing back at her daughter, she gave a little squeal. "The child is coming," she said. "Hurry! Help me!"

The attention of everyone in the room was drawn back immediately to the drama being played out before them.

Prince Chilpéric, third in line to the throne of Neustria, was born a few moments later, red and squalling. He let out a lusty yell as he was examined and pronounced hale and healthy. His mother smiled in relief as she bared her breast to his greedy little mouth.

"Thank you, Grandmamá," Laine whispered. "I knew something was wrong. I don't know what you did, but I suddenly felt a great burden lifted from my soul."

"Dearest child," Brisquayne said, gazing at the nativity scene with tears of joy in her faded old eyes. "I would never let any harm come to you."

She kept tight hold of her granddaughter with one hand, and made a sign against the Evil One with the other.

CHAPTER TWENTY-NINE

"'THE ROAD TO HELL IS LITTERED WITH GOOD INTENTIONS'"

That evening, the Princess Regent Arrhiána transited to the private alcove maintained in King Kipriyán's tent outside Saint Paulinos's Abbey, after waiting her turn for an hour in a line of couriers coming and going to Pommerelia. She refused to insert herself in front of anyone else who was waiting, saying that they had as much need or more than she, that they were all serving on the king's business.

Kipriyán himself had quarters in the monastery with the other royals, save Prince Arkády, who was using the king's tent as a command post.

"Sister!" the prince said, obviously happy to see her.

"Kásha," she responded, giving him a quick hug. "What news?"

He smiled down at her.

"We're in our usual state of organized chaos," he said. "However, both armies are now here, and we'll be ready to move forward again in two days. And sometime in the next week, Rhie, a battle will be won or lost on the road to Balíxira, and we'll know then who will be king next year in Pommerelia."

"I worry so much about you and Papá and our brothers," she said. "And there's nothing I can do except try to keep our spirits up in Paltyrrha as much as possible."

"Have you heard about Pulkhériya and Minérva being here?"

the prince asked.

"Yes," Arrhiána said, "but I still don't understand why."

"Pankratz allowed them to trail along behind him," Arkády said, "so now's there a big debate about whether to send them back or not. Of course, Cherie refuses to go, and Humfried is undecided what to do about it, as usual. I think Papá will at least insist that they remain here at Saint Paulinos's.

"How's everyone back home?" he added.

"As well as can be expected," she said. "You heard about Ari's most recent attack, I know, but he seems much better now. Doctor Melanthrix left some medication with us, and that's helped. Rÿna has become quite attached to the calling bell, which Dúra has allowed her to keep. Oh, and I've brought Sachette back to court for a while."

"I'm glad to hear it," he said.

"Well, that's really what I wanted to talk to you about," she said. "We had a prayer service this morning, and Chette saw something there that has greatly unsettled me. Perhaps I can best give you the nuances by sharing the experience with you directly. Link with me, brother."

She held out her slim hand, and he folded it within his larger, tanned, callused one, touching rings with her. Then she let her mind go blank, and began moving toward that state of sublime contemplation that signified a Psairothi mind at one with itself and the universe. It was like floating in a sea of serenity, a place where the self was enwrapped in an otherworldly glow, a sense that everything and nothing was possible at one and the same time, a feeling that there were greater things at work in the cosmos other than one's own petty concerns.

Arrhiána reached out through the leys and touched Arkády's soul, merging her senses with those of her older brother. Then she opened to him her memories of the encounter in Saint Konstantín's Cathedral. For a very long moment, the prince considered what he had seen.

This presence, for want of a better word, he said to her, *seems beneficent, even supportive of us, but I do not understand some of what he is saying. And yet, his "voice" seems familiar to me somehow, not in any direct fashion, but as something I've heard or seen or experienced peripherally, perhaps as a memory related to me by someone else. I can't place it yet, but I will. If we can trust him, it means we have an ally in our fight against our unseen killer.*

I've gone over the conversation time and again throughout the day, Arrhiána said, *and I believe very strongly that he wishes us well. I don't think that attitude could possibly have been faked, and Chette agrees with me. She had a much more prolonged encounter with whoever it was. Of course, what* he *thinks is good for us may not be the same as what* we *think. As the old saying goes, "the road to Hell is littered with good intentions." So I think we have to be cautious. And, of course, I don't know how to re-establish contact again. His reference to "coming to see him" is all well and good, but I still don't understand what he was talking about, and I certainly haven't figured out where "where" is yet.*

"Well, Rhie," Arkády said out loud, before adding mentally, *I'm sure you'll puzzle through it in your own good time. We've both been just a little busy with other matters these past weeks. Often, when I'm bedeviled by this kind of problem, I just let it simmer in the background, until the answer finally appears out of nowhere. The Lord will provide in His own good time.*

She abruptly kissed him on the cheek.

"So He will, dear brother," she said, "so He will. Now, I must get back to my duties in Paltyrrha, and I'm keeping you from your generals here in Pommerelia, whom I know need your direction. Arkády, please take care. I don't think I could bear the thought of living my life without you there. All of us need you. Kórynthia needs you. Come back home to us safe."

"That's not in my hands, Rhie," Arkády said. "But I'll try not to do anything more foolish than usual. You also be careful, sister. There's a madman loose among us. Don't let him catch you by surprise."

Then they hugged again, and she departed.

Lord Rónai, who had been waiting patiently in the vestibule, entered and saluted, simultaneously watching the princess exit.

"So what do you think, general?" Arkády asked.

The startled officer replied spontaneously, "She's quite a handsome woman, Highness."

Then, realizing what he had said, Rónai tried to apologize, but was cut short by the prince.

"Never mind," Arkády said, chuckling. "She *is* a handsome woman, and a handful, too, I suspect, for any man lucky enough to entrap her. So what do you have for me tonight?"

They worked long into the evening, going over troop dispositions and supply rations, while the candles burned down to merest nubs, and the lights began slowly going out around them, one by one, until none remained left to hold back the darkness.

CHAPTER THIRTY
"I HAVE SEEN THE FACE
OF HELL ON EARTH..."

THE HOMECOMING

"I have seen the face of Hell on earth," he said, gazing around at the rapt faces of his audience, "and it is called Killingford."

Three days earlier, the women working in the furthest fields of the Lordship of Ézion in Kosnick had noticed an aged, ragged pilgrim plodding slowly down the road from Kosnicksberg. He was bearded, dirty, and walked with a pronounced limp. His clothes were tattered, and he had a stained rag tied around his head to keep off the sun. A makeshift staff helped him make his painful way along the ruts of the dusty wagon tracks.

"Sárai," said Lady Nolána, who was pulling weeds with the rest of them, "go fetch a ladle of water for that poor old man. He looks half done in by the heat."

She straightened up, removed her broad-browed hat, and wiped the sweat off her face.

"Yes, milady," the girl said, hastening to the water trough. She was glad to have the break.

Nolána saw the servant carry a small bucket out to the traveler, and then suddenly drop it, putting both hands up to her face and giving a loud shriek.

"What is it?" her ladyship called out. "What...what's the matter?"

Turning to two of her companions, she said: "Jéna, Nikê,

grab your hoes and come with me."

They ran out to where the road entered the estate, and then down the lane to where Sárai was saying something to the pilgrim.

"Who are...?" Nolána started to speak from twenty feet away, and then the man looked up and her heart skipped a beat.

"Oh, God!" she exclaimed. "Oh God Almighty! Maury! Is it really you?"

She had no memory of running the rest of the way and throwing her arms around him.

"Maury!" she said. "Lord above, what's *happened* to you, my love?"

She had a hard time seeing through her tears.

"Ahh," he croaked, as if unused to speaking anything at all. He quickly drank down what little water remained in the bucket.

"Sárai," Nolána said, "go get some more water. Jéna, fetch the boys and Wyvin with the wagon. Quickly, quickly, now!"

To her husband, she said: "Lean on me, dearest, and I'll get you into the shade."

Finally he was able to respond to her original question.

"Have you heard naught of the war?" he asked.

"Just vague rumors of a battle out west somewhere," she said. "Nothing else."

"Then no one else has returned?" he asked.

"No one," Nolána said. "What is it, Maurin? What's happened? And where are your things?"

He sat down heavily under a tree.

"Too much to tell, my dear," he said, "to say it all now. I'm *so* tired. My only thought was reaching you, and now that I have, I have nothing else to give...."

Then he fell asleep, his head sliding sideways onto her shoulder, nor did he wake when Wyvin finally arrived with old Nobber leading the wagon.

He slept for sixteen hours straight, woke to eat some broth and bread and sip a little wine, and then went back again to bed. On the third day, he was pale and worn, but talking and acting more like his usual self. He called to his wife.

"Lána," he said, "I want you to send messages by courier to Countess Tirÿna, Lord Matán, Lady Pímay, Lady Zaménka, and the members of their respective families, asking them to join us here tomorrow afternoon. Then I'll tell everyone at once what I know about the Pommerelian campaign."

"Yes, husband," Nolána said.

That evening they shared the dinner meal together for the first time in three months.

"Lord," Maurin said, bowing his head and giving the invocation, "please bless this meal and honor this family. Accept our thanks for preserving my life and for showing me the way home. Grant Thy mercy unto those poor souls whose bodies now lie dead and unburied on the battlefield. Amen."

"Amen," his family said.

"Dáris," he said to his younger son, "please pass the bread and cheese."

At his insistence, they talked of ordinary things only, of how the crops were coming and which cows were a-milking and when the hot weather would break.

Afterwards, he sat with Nolána under a tree by the reservoir lake behind their house, sipping a cup of water, their backs propped against the bole of the great elm.

"I never thought to see you again," he said, "to be here like this, to view the ducks swimming upon the water, to revel in our children, to feel the brush of your hair against my face."

"Was it so awful?" she breathed quietly into his ear.

"You have no idea," he replied, shuddering visibly at the memory.

He put his arm around her shoulders and pulled her close.

"But this, this somehow makes it all worthwhile," he said, smelling the perfume of her breath.

The sun began to dip low behind the Carpates Mountains.

"The 'squitoes will be out soon," Maurin said. "Best to turn in."

"I'm in no hurry," Lána sighed. "Why don't we stay here a

while? It'll be dark soon, and Jéna will put the children to bed."

"What about *me*?" he said, chuckling.

"Oh, *I* will put *you* to bed," she whispered, kissing him.

"But I'm not sleepy," Maurin said.

"Nor am I," came the husky reply.

CHAPTER THIRTY-ONE
"MY NEWS IS NOT GOOD"

The Gathering

The next afternoon, their guests began to arrive. First came Tirÿna Countess of Kosnick and her two daughters, then Matán Lord Gándesa, and Pímay Lady Béçin, and Zaménka Lady Ya'os, plus their families and retainers, all of them members of or fiefs to the noble House of Kosnick. Other families from the immediate neighborhood also meandered through their gate as the afternoon progressed, bringing whatever spare food and drink they possessed, and helping in any way they could.

First they sat down to a feast of thanksgiving, the most sumptuous any of them had seen in a year, spread out on wooden tables near Lake Ézion, with over a hundred old men, women, and children participating. The atmosphere was subdued, since no one knew what had become of their menfolk, but they put as good a face upon the celebration as they could under the circumstance.

The children soon began to play along the shore, making up games to entertain themselves, and running and shouting to use up their spare energy. The adults watched quietly as the young ones laughed and the dogs barked in sheer enjoyment; the spectacle occasionally caused them to smile when they forgot themselves. A cool breeze began sweeping down from the nearby mountains late in the afternoon.

Finally, the moment they had all been waiting for arrived,

and the women began gathering their offspring, and settling them down in loose family groups in a large semicircle under the trees. Many of them spread blankets over the grass to make a place to sit; the nobility picked separate spots just for themselves and theirs, while the rest of the folk intermingled.

Then Lord Maurin von Markstadt stepped to the center of the half-circle, and faced the multitude.

"You all know who am I," he said, "and I know you. We've spent most of our lives together. Since it appears that I am the first of the Kosnicki men to find his way home, I have an obligation to tell you what happened out there, and what it was like. As you may have guessed, my news is not good."

A low moan emanated from the assembled families, and some of the women held their children close.

"I do not have all of the answers that you seek," he said, "except to tell you that others will almost certainly be following in my wake. I don't know exactly how many, and in many cases, I don't know exactly who. Where I have answers, I'll give them to you honestly and straightforwardly."

CHAPTER THIRTY-TWO
"...AND IT IS CALLED KILLINGFORD"

THE PRELUDE

Lord Maurin paused for a moment, as if pondering where to begin. He wiped the sweat dripping from his brow.

"I have seen the face of Hell on earth," he intoned, gazing around at the rapt faces of his audience, "and it is called Killingford.

"We left Paltyrrha on the first day of May, marching west towards the mountains. Although the rains were often heavy and the roads muddy, we made good time, and reached Mylåßgorod without incident two weeks later. I met a funny little monk named Father Athanasios on the way, and we traveled much of the distance together, entertaining each other with our stories.

"Our boys were good and ready for a fight, let me tell you, and drilled together as well as any unit I ever saw. Count Dónan kept everyone in line, but our brigade disciplined itself, if you know what I mean, because they believed in the righteousness of our cause.

"On the third night out, I was introduced to Prince Arkády, as good a commander as I've ever met, plus several of his brothers. Prince Nikolaí, the next youngest of the Tighrishi, was a big, burly warrior whose accomplishments were championed constantly by the men.

"I was not as impressed with the new Pommerelian king,

who seemed to me overwhelmed with his new position and his own importance, and who didn't show as much consideration for his own soldiers as the Tighrishi did.

"Myláßgorod was a mess. Our campground was full of mud and bugs, the provisions were spotty, and we were stuck there for several days. Finally, they moved us out early one morning. We had scarcely marched a mile towards the pass when word came that Prince Nikolaí had conquered the Pommerelian fort at the top. Now, that victory cheered us up a great deal, and we pushed forward with even greater vigor than before.

"It took us two days to traverse the mountains. There we set up temporary camp while the engineers built several devices on the cliff overlooking Borgösha, the Pommerelian fortress rooted down below. The next day they started lobbing huge stones over the wall, one of which, we learned later, killed their commander, the local count. The city was abandoned the next day, and we moved in immediately.

"We rousted out the spies and anti-Psairothi elements right quickly, that's for sure, and lined their heads upon the city walls like so many pennants. King Kipriyán called that afternoon for a ceremony of accession, and we all gathered 'round the main town square, which had a huge elm tree right in the center. There King Humfried was proclaimed ruler of Pommerelia, and his son Prince Pankratz, who was up north commanding the Bolémi army, made Hereditary Prince. It was a grand sight.

"But then a storm came up suddenly as Humfried was making his lengthy speech, and lightning struck the great tree, splitting a branch loose. King Kipriyán was knocked senseless, and his chief physician, Fra Jánisar Cantárian, was crushed by the falling limb. The funeral for those who had perished at Borgösha, among them Cantárian, was held the very next day, with the patriarch himself presiding. At the same time, the papist Church of Saint Catalina the Centonist was reconsecrated as Saint Michaêl's Cathedral, with the Protopresbyter Varlaám Njégosh being named the new bishop there. The Romanish clergy were given the opportunity of swearing allegiance to the Orthodox Church; those who refused were banished to the west. The conversion of Pommerelia to the true faith had finally begun.

"We spent several more days encamped outside the city, waiting for the rest of the army to clear the Skopélosz Pass. Then we proceeded slowly up the valley of the Spargö River to the fortress of Karkára. Although there were occasional attacks by Pommerelian irregulars on our left flank, the river helped to protect our forces, and we sloughed off their minor raids like a dog shakes off fleas.

"Karkára was a much tougher problem. Its position and height made it almost impregnable except for a prolonged siege from the Kórynthi side, where the flat valley floor permitted the great engines to be brought to bear on the twenty-foot stone walls. We tried several assaults from the Pommerelian side, but the steep canyon there put us at a great disadvantage. Finally, Prince Kiríll devised a plan whereby he would take a small force from Westmark up the canyon of the Vá'al, which allowed access to the relatively undefended north side of the fortress. Our brigade was one of those delegated to wait in the canyon below for Kiríll's men to open the main gates.

"The attack was a great success. Using homemade ladders, Prince Kiríll was able to scale the northern walls undetected, and take the guardhouse over the main gate. Before the Pommerelians could react, Kiríll's rangers had winched the portcullis far enough up where our men could start squeezing through. I'm proud to say that the Kosnicki troops acquitted themselves very well that day. We penetrated straight to the citadel, and cut down the Pommerelian commander, at which point all resistance ended. We had taken the last great castle before Balíxira!

"It took us several days to regroup, during which time we received the disappointing news of Duke Ferdinand's defeat in the west, although we had never really counted on his support. As in Borgösha, Patriarch Avraäm soon sent the Latinate clergy packing, reconsecrating the old church of Saint Tyrranus under its new name of Saint Innokénty.

"And then we were heading northwest, 'round the point of the Läuterung Highlands, where we were supposed to meet Prince Ezzö's army coming down from Einwegflasche. We had already heard that Lockenlöd Castle had been taken and its count killed, so we knew our boys were well on their way south.

"We stopped at a small abbey called Saint Paul's, an establishment of the Verbenans, one of the more popular religious orders in Pommerelia, known especially for their gaily colored gardens and bright, yellow-and-green robes. We appropriated it as a command center after the monks had fled, leaving their trowels in place, since the compound was ideally located to service the supply columns coming from the north, the east, and the southeast, and set up camp around it. The patriarch immediately reconsecrated the chapel there to honor the name of Saint Paulinos the Persecuted, who had died a martyr to the Orthodox faith at the hands of the papists.

"On the next day, the eleventh of June, Prince Ezzö's column arrived from the north, and the army was reunited. I tell you, it was a grand sight to see thirty thousand Kórynthi soldiers encamped in Pommerelia, ready to lay siege first to Balíxira and then to Rabestadt. King Kyprianos spoke to us the next day, exhorting us to do our best for the honor of Kórynthia and the glory of our families. Then Holy Patriarch Avraäm blessed everyone, and called upon God to endorse our great enterprise. We marched south two days later, flags flying in the breeze, a brave bunch of boys heading off to war.

"On the next day, we encountered a group of outriders from the Pommerelian army, who raided our scouting parties and then attacked our front units, but rode rapidly off when pressed. King Kipriyán held us back, wisely not allowing the different corps to get spread apart where they might be vulnerable to another attack. All day we had been following a fast, deep river called the Falling Water, which runs directly south to Balíxira.

"That night there was a great council of war, with all of the major officers discussing our various military options. Quite a number of our scouts had been killed earlier that day in the raid, including Sir Léka d'Örs, who knew the terrain better than anyone else, so we were without his valuable contributions. We thought we might encounter the main Pommerelian force sometime in the next few days, that they couldn't let us get too close to Balíxira without making at least some effort to stop us. We knew that we outnumbered them by at least ten thousand men, so the general opinion was that we ought to close as quickly as possible, that such a conflict would be decisive, effectively ending the war. We were wrong."

CHAPTER THIRTY-THREE
"THIS HERE'S THE SCHILLING-FORD"

THE FIRST DAY: THE FEAST OF SAINT OUITOS

Lord Maurin cleared his throat, and paused long enough to take a long swig from a winesack. Then he asked for a stool, saying: "You will pardon me, gentlefolk, but my leg still troubles me."

After he had found a comfortable position beneath a spreading chestnut tree, he continued with his story.

"At dawn on the next day, we broke camp as usual and resumed our march south. The skies were cloudless and the weather unseasonably hot. We had been having trouble finding sufficient supplies of good water for the last two days, since the walls of the river canyon were too steep to traverse easily, and the local creeks seemed to be drying up in the sun.

"For some hours that morning we saw nothing more than the usual distant outriders of the enemy, which we could neither touch nor stop, any more than they could ours, although I now believe that the attack against our scouts on the previous day had been a deliberate attempt by the Pommerelians to blind us to our surroundings.

"About midday there was a commotion behind us, near the end of the column, and I looked back to see a large dust cloud appear on our left flank. They had waited until much of our army had passed them by, and then attacked our rear, rolling up our trailing units like so much broken kindling.

"Their archers and infantry had been secreted in a hidden rill that ran parallel to our forces for about a mile or so, and they had simultaneously sent out their cavalry to attack our supply train. I could soon see the smoke from our burning wagons intermingling with the dust whirls. Such is the advantage of knowing the terrain in which one must fight.

"Although chaos reigned everywhere at first, Prince Nikolaí rallied our cavalry, who rode at full speed back along both sides of our lines. The enemy horsemen immediately broke off their attack when they saw our brave boys coming, and headed for cover to the east. When Nikolaí's forces tried to follow, they were stopped with a barrage of arrows from a row of well-positioned archers, and had to withdraw until we could bring up our own men to support them. I estimate that he lost one-quarter of his horsemen to death or injury in that first barrage, plus several hundred mounts.

"Prince Arkády had not been idle during this time, and he was already trying to restore order to our badly disrupted rear guard, sending several brigades northeast to roust the enemy archers, and halting the main army's advance. He ordered the lead units to wheel ponderously around in a circle, in order to cut off any escape to the southeast.

"Their longbowmen created havoc in our lines. As I have already mentioned, these archers had been hidden in a crack in the earth that had apparently been artificially widened and deepened, and they were almost impregnable until we were able to attack in force with our infantry. As we began to bring more of our might to bear on the Pommerelian lines, the enemy slowly withdrew under pressure, falling back to what I now believe were a series of previously-established retreat positions. They were taking very few casualties, while we were forced to advance through completely open fields covered with dry grass. The slaughter was immense.

"Nonetheless, our brave boys continued to force the Pommerelians back towards a low ridge looming to the left of our line, or due east from our main army. No one gave any thought as to what this rocky formation might indicate. The enemy fought well, but we outnumbered them by a considerable measure, and as more of our brigades joined the fray, our progress was inexorable.

"The lay of the land tended gradually upwards as the Pommerelians successively retreated from position to position. We were now able to use some of their own trenches to provide cover to our bowmen and infantry, and this helped us considerably. We never thought that the attackers represented anywhere near the full force of the Pommerelian army, and we presumed, wrongly as it turned out, that we had merely encountered a larger than normal raiding party.

"By mid-afternoon, we had pushed them back to the ridge itself. Suddenly there appeared above us at least a thousand archers working from well-established and -chosen positions, who laid down a barrage such as I have never seen. The very sun was darkened with the flight of arrows that peppered our forces, and at least a thousand of our men now lay dying or injured before the Pommerelian lines. The very ground seemed to have sprouted a field of feathered sticks. I'm sorry to say, Lady Tirÿna, that your son, Hereditary Count Amánty, was one of the casualties there."

Maurin bowed his head in sorrow.

"Oh, God, no!" the Countess Kosnick exclaimed. She quietly began to sob, and was comforted by her daughters and Lady Nolána.

Maurin sipped again from his winesack, and then continued.

"He was but the first of the many brave Kosnicki that I saw die that day. We fell back. We had no choice: it was either retreat or be slaughtered. We regrouped outside the range of those deadly bows, and the officers held an impromptu meeting to decide on our next strategy.

"'What's on the other side of that ridge?' Prince Arkády asked. 'Can we get around it?'

"The man Çévik, now chief scout after the death of Sir Léka, stepped forward.

"'I believe it's the river again, highness,' he said. 'We've been following it off and on for about twenty miles. The ridge should drop off steeply on the other side into the gorge, if it holds to pattern. Unfortunately, those of us who knew anything about this particular area were killed yesterday, so I can't give you any more detailed information.'

"'I hate committing our men without knowing what's on the other side,' the prince said. 'Send out scouts to the north and south along the ridge, and capture any of the locals that you can find. Bring them back for questioning.'

"Then Prince Nikolaí spoke up.

"'I believe we should disengage,' he said, 'and continue our advance on Balíxira.'

"'We can't leave an enemy force this large behind us,' King Kipriyán said.

"'If we move on,' Nikolaí said, 'they'll be forced to engage us on open ground, where we have an advantage in numbers. Here, we're being chewed to pieces.'

"But the king's counsel prevailed, and they quickly decided to press the attack against the Pommerelian army. Four of the catapults were hastily assembled, and loaded with loose rocks. As soon as they were in place, the Altorfi Brigade moved forward. I could see the sun reflecting off their spear points as line after line of determined soldiers marched their way up that hill. Again came the whir of the arrow shower, followed by the 'thunk, thunk' of our engines flinging their stones at the Pommerelian lines, and the screams of those on the receiving end. Our bowmen also let fly their bolts, and soon I could hear the cries of hundreds of wounded men.

"The black-suited Altorfi flung their long spears as one, pulled their flashing swords from their scabbards, and marched doubletime straight at the Walküri battlements. Only a quarter of those who started up that long rise ever reached the top, and then they were locked in a nasty, hand-on-hand struggle to the death. We couldn't see from below much of what was happening, until the dust cleared enough to reveal the Pommerelian lines still holding, and grotesque piles of bodies littering the slope in front of them. We groaned together as one.

"Then it was our turn, together with the Südmarki Brigade. I left my mount below, and we marched side by side up that long hill, jumping over the ditches and landing on the bodies of our comrades. All around us were the prone figures of wounded soldiers pleading for a cup of water, and the many others who were past anyone's help. The stench was overpowering, and the flies buzzed around us by the thousands. We could hear the catapults working again to either side, trying to blast a way through the Pommerelian battlements for us.

"Then the arrows came, raining down on us like hordes of buzzing insects, pricking the blood out of those unfortunate enough to be bit by them. My aide Sülçis, who was marching right beside me, was suddenly struck down by two bolts hitting him in the chest and arm. He died almost instantly. Lord Gándesa, I'm sorry to tell you that I also saw your son, Hereditary Lord Khrysór, hit by an arrow in the leg, but I don't know if he lived or died that day; I never saw him again afterwards.

"Above us we heard a terrible rumbling noise, and I saw several huge stones rolling down the slope toward us, obviously purposely dislodged. Those who were struck by them were instantly killed. They continued cutting through the troops behind us until they reached the bottom of the hill. As we crossed over one abandoned ditch, I noticed a black substance in the bottom. Then several fire arrows hit close around us, igniting the dark oil in the ditch, and burning some of the soldiers immediately following us. Their screams were terrible to hear.

"We had decided to retain our spears until the end, and when we finally reached the top of the ridge, we used them to impale the defenders and push them back over the other side. Then the enemy cavalry was there, pricking us with their lances, and a free-for-all ensued. In the end, though, our brave men carried the day, and just as the sun was starting to set, the enemy withdrew down the opposite slope toward the river. When we had a chance to catch our breath, we could see that the drop-off here was not nearly as steep as it had been further up the river canyon.

"We could not pursue them. Less than half of our two brigades had survived the charge, and we were totally exhausted from the struggle. Much to my surprise, before the sun went down completely, I saw some of the retreated Pommerelians splashing across the Falling Water River without difficulty. I also noticed a cluster of huts along our side of the river bank.

"Early that evening we were replaced by fresh troops who occupied the ridge, and allowed us to regroup back to the camp, where we managed to find something warm to eat. The officers were then called to another war council.

"'What are our losses?' asked good King Kipriyán.

"Prince Nikolaí said: 'We lost four or five thousand men today, and the enemy just five hundred or a thousand, no more. They've stung us, no question. However, we now have the ridge and we should have the advantage tomorrow.'

"Prince Arkády ordered the chief scout to bring someone forward, and we could spy a scruffy old herdsman being led by a rope around his neck.

"'Who are you?' the prince asked.

"'Just a sheepherder, milord,' the carle said. 'Folks 'round here call me Hal.'

"'What *is* this place, Hal?' Arkády inquired.

"'This here's the Schilling-Ford, sir,' the herdsman responded. 'Lived here all me life, I have.'

"'Then the river is passable here?' the prince said.

"'Aye, lord,' the old man said. 'So 'tis. Only place youse can get yerself acrost, for a long ways up and down the creek, like, 'cept durin' Ogust, maybe.'

"'Where's the Pommerelian army?' Nikolaí asked.

"'Dunno, lord,' Hal said. 'Been out with mah sheep for weeks. Dunno nothin' 'bout stuff like that. Youse the first folks I seen 'n a long time.'

"We were all reading the man with our *psai*-rings, and could see that he was telling the truth. Various lords and generals questioned him further, before they finally gave up in disgust. He was obviously a simpleton. We did find out that the village of Schilling had perhaps two dozen inhabitants, none of them very prosperous, and that the road was terrible, which perhaps accounted for the small amount of traffic that it saw.

"Ultimately, the king decided to press forward with the attack. If this *was* the main Pommerelian army—and some of us were still not convinced—then it was imperative that we find some way of destroying or damaging it as a fighting force.

"We went to sleep that night confident of our victory on the morrow. Far better, I now think, if we had all had nightmares about the days to come."

CHAPTER THIRTY-FOUR
"ANOTHER HOT DAY"

THE SECOND DAY: THE FEAST OF SAINT KOUIRIKOS

"The next morning promised to be another hot day. Even at sunrise there was a heaviness to the air that boded high temperatures by noon, or possibly sooner. We were a somber lot as we stowed our gear away, perhaps for the last time, and checked our weapons. I grieved for our lost comrades, but I knew that we had a hard day's fighting ahead if we were to prevail.

"The patriarch blessed us after we had broken our fast, and promised us Heaven if we fought well. That comforted some, but worried others. The royal princes all went to their battle corps, in preparation for beginning the march. During the night, crews had removed the dead and injured to the rear, burying the corpses in a common grave, except for the officers, and tending to the wounded with the military doctors.

"Some of the officers trod their way up the slope again to the ridge, to espy what the enemy was doing, and to see the lay of the land. Down below was the small village, its houses, if one could call them that, scattered randomly along the near bank of the Falling Water River. The stream broadened here to more than twice the width that it had in the rest of the gorge, obviously making the depth considerably less in the process. The slope on the opposite bank, like the one on our side, was also less steep than usual for this canyon, with rolling hills just beyond, and highlands in the distance. We could see some Pommerelian emplacements here and there, but the details and numbers were unclear. There were also some soldiers or officers lined on the opposite ridge examining *us*, which was no great surprise.

"We had decided the previous night that the campaign would be managed from one of the old Pommerelian emplacements on our ridge, and that the two kings would remain there to direct operations. We were ready to march two hours after sunrise.

"Since our boys had been bloodied on the previous afternoon, the Kosnicki Brigade was held in reserve this day, and several fresh units were ordered to take the point. Their spears had been stowed, since the soldiers would only be hampered by them in trying to cross the ford, and they had been issued shields instead to help protect against the arrows.

"Five thousand men moved down the slope as one unit. My heart soared at the sight, for I knew that we couldn't be defeated this day. The first ranks plunged into the cold river water, and then our men started falling for no apparent cause, jumping up and down in rage and frustration. The entire brigade came to a halt. We officers strained our eyes trying to see what was wrong. A messenger came galloping back up the slope.

"'What is it?' King Humfried asked, obviously impatient.

"The scout paled.

"'They're being stung, sire,' he said.

"'What?' he yelled. 'Pankratz,' he said, 'get down there and find out what's going on.'

"Meanwhile, the entire army had stopped, bunching up on the shore, the units losing their order. Suddenly hundreds of yeomen appeared out of another ditch on the Pommerelian side of the stream, and loosed thousands of arrows on the unsuspecting troops. Our men began to bolt back uphill.

"'Stop them!' shouted Humfried.

"It took another hour to get the situation back under control. King Humfried insisted on having every twentieth man in his corps executed for cowardice. This greatly disheartened our troops. We did not need to lose any more men from our own actions.

"Finally, Prince Pankratz rode up with a partial explanation. Without saying a word, he handed his father a thin slab of wood studded with sharp iron spikes. Evidently, sappers had been carefully laying the things for the last several days, completing the task the previous night, by filling in the lanes they had left vacant for their own escape.

"After the infernal device had been handed around to the officers, the prince said: 'We've also discovered some longer spikes, spears really, jammed into the deeper pools of the streambed. There's no easy way to find and remove them manually.'

"We heard a commotion down below, and rushed over the edge. Some of the Pommerelian soldiers had pulled down their pantaloons and were taunting our boys with their bare buttocks, a wholly disreputable display of unprofessional behavior. They finally stopped when one of our yeoman stung one in the ass with a long shot from his bow.

"We spent some time then discussing the impasse, and had almost decided to withdraw and head for Balíxira when Doctor Melanthrix appeared, and examined the spikes.

"'These were made of metal,' he said, 'so they would remain on the bottom long enough to have some effect. Even so, it will not be long before some of them begin moving out of position. Already they may have shifted. We have a way to counter this.'

"King Kipriyán smiled then, and a terrible thing it was to see. It was like the great gray wolf who suddenly realizes that his prey lies naked and vulnerable before him, and begins panting in anticipation.

"'Do it!' he said.

"Then the magician went back to his tent, and brought back some powders and phials and a book of spells. He stood on the highest point of the ridge and began chanting in a tongue I did not recognize, while simultaneously sprinkling powder over something in his left hand. Then he opened his fingers, and I saw that he held a small magnet there, nestled between his rings. He raised the metal on high, displaying it where the rays of the sun could strike it, and with his right hand threw down a phial that exploded with a burst of green light.

"'*Fiat lux!*' he cried, 'like unto like,' and the magnet seemed to pulsate with an aura of sunlight.

"Again he dashed a phial upon the rocks below, and it flashed a vibrant red.

"'*Fiat magnes!*' he chanted, 'like unto like,' and the stone began to hum.

"Finally, he threw a third phial down the slope, breaking it in a sudden display of violet light.

"'*Fiat ferrum!*' he shouted, and the water in the river began to bubble and boil as if it were a cauldron. Suddenly we could see black dots rising from the surface of the stream, and I knew these were the spikes that had stopped our men from crossing. Fifty feet into the air he raised them, and then dashed them all at once upon the Pommerelian lines.

"There were screams of anguish and shouts of surprise on the slope across from us, as the enemy soldiers were subjected to one of their own tricks. I do not think the Walküri suffered very many casualties from Melanthrix's attack, but they certainly took a blow to their pride. For the first time in two days, we howled with laughter at the enemy's discomfiture.

"The magician Melanthrix, however, had to be helped down from his perch, so tired was he. It had taken great power to leverage so much iron from the running water, but he had done it. Would that he had not.

"Already our brigades were moving back into position. The kings gave the order to move forward, and for the second time that day, our brave soldiers marched gaily into battle, pennants flying. This time, however, when they reached the river, they plunged right into the water, and nothing stopped them other than the clouds of pesky arrows that continued to nag our men. It barely slowed us down.

"More and more troops crowded down towards the shore, as our boys began to climb up the opposite bank. Strangely, however, they encountered no Pommerelian opposition other than the flying bolts. Perhaps, we thought, this was indeed only a harassing force. We should have been more careful.

"The first indication was a distant rumbling noise, like a bear growling over a bad meal that had disturbed his stomach. I felt a deep vibration in the ground unlike anything I have ever encountered save the Paltyrrha temblor. We all began looking around at each other, trying to see what the trouble might be, when Prince Norbert shouted wildly, pointing upstream. There, coming rapidly 'round the bend, was a ten-foot wall of water. We determined later that the Pommerelians had dammed one of the small tributaries of the Falling Water a week or two before, in anticipation of this day.

"Our boys strove mightily to retreat up the slope, but in the press and confusion, only a fraction managed to escape. The flood swept away three or four thousand men, most of whom were drowned, plus all of the huts that constituted the village of Schilling. Although we rescued a few survivors a mile or two downstream, many of those who escaped were captured by the Pommerelians."

Lord Maurin shook his head, and wiped a tear away.

"My friends, it is one thing to be killed honorably in the heat of battle, to have faced one's opponent squarely and to have won or lost on the throw of the die. Every soldier lives with this possibility from the first day he enlists. But to perish so meaninglessly.... We then thought the Pommerelians the most dishonorable opponents we had ever faced, worse even than the barbarian hordes of Åvarsland, who at least allowed a man to die with dignity.

"There was no retreating now. The men wouldn't hear of it. For us it had become a blood feud, something that we could not let rest until one side or the other was destroyed. Both kings agreed: this would be a battle to the death, with no holds barred.

"Curiously, though, there was a lull in the fighting. Our men were fed their midday meal and thoroughly watered, and we saw some of the Pommerelians doing the same. In early afternoon the trumpets blared again for assembly, and five thousand men prepared to march forward into death. I was still on the ridge with the officers, and I could hear the beat of the drums as the brave soldiers of Kórynthia strode down that slope towards the river.

"The five thousand reached the retamed ford, and there they met five thousand Pommerelians head-on, right in the middle of the water. For our enemy now understood exactly what this struggle was about, and they had determined to commit their entire force, if necessary, to prevent us from advancing further.

"It was like two wrestlers of equal weight and skills, matched against each other in the ring, with neither willing to give even an inch to the other, and no time limit to the match. Back and forth the tide of battle surged, and the Falling Water turned red with the blood of the soldiers. From our vantage point we could see the stain flowing downstream, spreading ever further as the afternoon progressed. Gradually the fighting diminished as both sides neared exhaustion, and the tattered remnants of the two brigades slowly withdrew to their respective sides of the Falling Water. No advantage had been gained."

* * * * * * *

"In mid-afternoon the kings decided to commit our main force. Prince Nikolaí's cavalry had proved ineffectual in the fight due to the confined space available to him, and so his men dismounted, their horses being taken to the rear. From this point on they would fight as foot soldiers with the rest of us.

"The Kosnicki Brigade also prepared to march, under the leadership of Count Dónan. After the previous day's clash, we were only at half strength, but we would not be left behind. Prince Norbert was delegated to command the rear guard at the abbey up north. The Kórynthi army was prepared to take the Schilling-Ford.

"By this point we had concluded that we were indeed facing all or most of the main Pommerelian army. Too many troops had been committed by our enemy for this to be a mere raiding party, and we had spotted amongst their officers men whom we believed to be high-ranking officials of state; one of our boys with exceptional sight had even identified King Barnim at his command post atop the far ridge.

"I was watching the same high ground, when I noticed some activity across the valley, which I pointed out to Prince Arkády. Silently we observed streams of Pommerelian soldiers coming off the ridge, and assembling on the slope in front of it. Also, I noticed clusters of men doing other things that were not clear; they were partially hidden by the rocks along the top.

"At last came the order to proceed, and I rejoined my fellow Kosnicki as Subcommander, now second in rank in our brigade only to the count himself. Fifteen thousand soldiers, in waves of five thousand each, began to march in file towards the lost village of Schilling. On the opposite slope, an equal number of Pommerelians started down the other side.

"Suddenly, the enemy ridge blossomed with a row of great engines dragged up from behind, and these let loose a barrage of large and small rocks, as well as huge fireballs. Our forces were so densely packed that these missiles caused great havoc amongst our soldiers. I saw one huge stone hit ten feet in front of me, squashing the men there like so many ants. It bounced over my head and landed again somewhere behind me, rolling off to one side, and then back down the slope when its momentum was spent, mowing over a line of fighters in both directions. Our own machines opened fire on the enemy forces, and started chewing up the Pommerelian soldiers.

"The armies met again in midstream, where the swirling current and slippery underrocks made fighting especially treacherous. The water here was three or four feet deep in places, just fast enough to sweep one's legs away under the right conditions, and bitterly cold. So many men were crammed into such a small space that the dead sometimes remained standing until the mass of soldiers around them shifted, allowing them to fall. The ford was about a half-mile in width, but at its furthest edges contained deep holes that could swallow a man in an instant. This became less of a problem as the afternoon waned, as the spaces began filling with dead bodies, giving the survivors better footing.

"I found myself facing a huge Pommerelian officer who outweighed me by several stone. The first big swing of his sword hit my shield so hard that my whole left arm went numb. I knew that death had come unless I could somehow outthink the man. My only advantage was the lack of maneuverability on both sides. On his next swing, I angled my shield so his sword would penetrate it partway. Then, putting all my strength into the motion, I yanked backwards with my left arm and body, pulling him slightly off balance. He was unable to get his own shield back into position before I ran him through the left side.

"I finished him with a second blow, but lingered too long over my victory. I felt a blade cut into my right thigh, and would have died right there, I think, if my swordmate hadn't cut the attacker down. I almost drowned in the cold water trying to get back to the shore. Several times I had to defend myself, but managed to push my attacker back long enough to escape.

"The battle had now degenerated into a *mêlée* of man against man, or sometimes cluster against cluster. When I reached the bank, I pulled myself up onto the mud, and was dragged away by the doctors' assistants back up the slope, and taken over the ridge to our temporary camp. As an officer, I received first treatment from the available physicians. My wound was cleaned and bandaged, but I had lost a great deal of blood, and was ordered to remain on the ridge. From there I watched the rest of the great battle.

"I saw both Count Dónan and Makhtár Lord Ya'os carried to the medical tents. I followed them in, but there was nothing anyone could do for Lord Ya'os, I am sorry to say, milady; he was dead before he arrived."

Lord Maurin bowed solemnly in her direction, but Lady Zaménka was inconsolable.

"Also killed this day was Prince Nikolaí, who took an axe meant for his brother, Prince Arkády. I did not see this myself, but heard about it later. Count Dónan was severely injured from multiple wounds," Maurin continued, "but he survived the day, and although he lost his right arm, he appeared well on the way to recovery.

"From the bluffs I watched the fighting continue. Neither side could pass the ford. Thousands of bodies of the dead and dying littered the ground, while others were gradually being swept downstream. As the sun began to set, the soldiers finally withdrew to their respective camps, most of them collapsing there without eating. I believe ten thousand men were killed in this one struggle, with casualties about equal on both sides.

"Later that night, we officers were again called to the war council; there were many fewer of us left by this point. I had been named commander of the remnants of the Kosnicki Brigade until Count Dónan could return to duty. I appointed his two surviving sons, Lords Marón and Ambrósim, as my deputies, and all three of us attended the meeting.

"The arguments that evening proved as fierce as the battles we had already fought. Some, such as Prince Arkády, believed we should withdraw, that we only had eight or ten thousand effective fighting men left, which was insufficient to take the great citadel of Balíxira, even if we won this battle. But King Kipriyán and King Humfried wouldn't hear of retreat, and insisted that we push the conflict to its bitter end. In truth, our losses had been horrendous, far greater than anyone would have believed. I did not think that the 'luck' was with us anymore.

"In the end, we lesser officers were dismissed to bed, and the handful of senior men remained to discuss some other alternative which they didn't want us to hear. We only learned the results of their deliberations the next day.

"I slept poorly that night, my sleep being filled with nightmares of giant Pommerelians coming at me with their greatswords. Morning came far too quickly."

CHAPTER THIRTY-FIVE
"A BRILLIANT FLASH
OF GREEN LIGHT"

THE THIRD DAY: THE FEAST OF SAINT BÓTOULPHOS

Lord Maurin von Markstadt then requested a short break. He got up and stretched his legs and helped himself to a ladle of fresh water from the nearby spring, washing the taste of stale wine out of his mouth, before sitting back down again and resuming his narrative.

"The next morning, strangely, we were allowed to take our time getting started. The men finally assembled about *tritê*, or more than three hours after sunrise. This caused a great deal of comment in the ranks, which we officers soon put a stop to, believe me. Then King Kipriyán asked to address us all.

"'Brave soldiers of Kórynthia,' his voice boomed down from his vantage point on the ridge, 'victory will be ours today. You have all fought with great distinction here, and we will not sacrifice your lives needlessly. Therefore, we have decided to trick the tricksters with a magical working, which will frighten them into retreat and give us the edge we need to finish them for good. This will be a glorious day in the history of Kórynthia, and you will make it happen. *For honor and Kórynthia!*,' he added.

"'*For honor and Kórynthia!*' we yelled.

"Then we moved out, marching from our camp up over the ridge and down the slope on the other side again. We stopped short of the point where the Pommerelian catapults could reach us. The remaining enemy troops assembled in force on the opposite side of the river. I thought I saw a glint of gold off the crown of King Barnim, who had now joined his men for what they assumed was the final battle.

"Prince Arkády and Prince Zakháry rode out to our right and left, placing at each spot a strange, upright, metallic structure with branches sprouting out the top. King Humfried and Prince Pankratz took up their position with another device just in front of us, centered exactly between the other two princes. Behind us on the ridge, King Kipriyán began working a fourth engine with the assistance of Doctor Melanthrix and Prince Ezzö.

"The first sign that we had of anything being different was a change in the quality of the light. It was as if someone had placed a tinted pane of glass over the sun. The air cooled noticeably, and a light wind began to swirl in the canyon. Suddenly I could hear a chanting coming from the kings and the princes. The hair on the back of my neck rose.

"Gradually the wind became stronger and the sunlight dimmer. Men in both armies looked around at each other to find some comfort in their company. I was standing close to Prince Arkády's position on the left side of the front line.

"There was a sudden crackling in the air. Small bolts of green lightning began emanating from the metallic devices, reaching into the sky. Then Prince Arkády's engine connected to King Humfried's with a bolt of energy, and soon all had linked, one unto the others. It seemed to me as if the focus of the working was set at the central machine in front, for there the energies were obviously greater.

"Some of our men began shrinking back away from the huge discharges that were emptying into the sky, but I kept my place. I'm a Kosnicki and a Markstadt, and I don't retreat from danger.

"A large emerald ball began forming above King Humfried's device. It rotated above us, gleaming with green light and shot through with continual bursts of lightning. It seemed to me as if the other points of the nexus were funneling energy into the thing, making it increase in size at a steady pace.

"Then something went wrong. I don't pretend to understand exactly what they were trying to do, or how it was constituted, or the hazards involved, although I'm certain they were great. These were Psairothi adepts, and they knew better than I whether they could accomplish what they set out to do. I can only give you my impressions.

"King Humfried shouted something to his son, and I saw Prince Pankratz's pale features as he turned to gesture at someone up on our ridge. Then the ball began to rotate even faster as it drifted higher into the air, discharging bolts of energy randomly over the battlefield. One of these struck one of our men, knocking him dead.

"Prince Pankratz made an adjustment to their engine, and yelled something to his father. King Humfried was making wild motions with his hands, his rings almost incandescent with the light, chanting a series of words that were drowned in the static given off by the green globe. By this time the orb had drifted to the center of the river, hanging about fifty feet off the surface. The Pommerelians were starting to run back up the opposite slope, and some of our men had also retreated.

"A brilliant flash of green light from the ball struck Humfried and his son in their hands, burning them up where they stood. I think they must have died instantly. The links between the devices vanished, and the orb began to pulsate. Suddenly, bolts of emerald energy started shooting from the globe in every direction, striking the men on both sides at random.

"I knew then the thing was out of control. I knelt down in the dust, quickly centered myself, and erected a screen of protection with my *ley*-ring, making my profile as small as possible to get the maximum benefit. I closed my eyes and covered my face, turning my back to the orb.

"Then everything exploded. I was blown over and over, rolling at least twenty or thirty feet. Around me men were covered in flames, trying desperately to put out the emerald fires that were consuming them. Most died horribly.

"For a moment I blacked out. When I came to, I somehow managed to stand up. Everything seemed strangely silent, until I realized I was temporarily deaf. Both slopes of the valley were blackened from the discharge. Thousands of corpses littered the ground, often frozen in grotesque positions, one or more limbs jutting in the air. Not far from me, Prince Arkády came to his feet. His hair was singed, and he was covered with soot, but like me, he had had the presence of mind to create a protective spell.

"The killing fields of Killingford—there was no other name more appropriate—had claimed the lives of at least forty thousand men, including fifteen thousand or more on the last day alone. Those who survived were either protected by the ridge or by the bodies of their fellow soldiers or by ditches, only a few having the knowledge and the presence to save themselves in other ways.

"I wearily began helping those few men who had survived the conflagration, and I could see the survivors on the other slope doing the same. We paid no more attention to each other, either on that day or on the next. The war was over, and everyone knew it."

CHAPTER THIRTY-SIX
"NOT MUCH ELSE TO TELL"

THE RETREAT

Tears were streaming down Lord Maurin's face, as they were on the cheeks of almost everyone listening to him. Even the children were unexpectedly somber, perhaps understanding in some vital way that their parents needed a temporary respite from their demands.

Finally, he regained sufficient control of himself to continue.

"There is not much else to tell," he said. "We spent two days there trying to recover the wounded and to identify the dead. Except for the royals and the major officers, who were preserved in brine for the trip home, all of the men were buried in common graves. Thank the Lord that the King Kipriyán and his sons, the Princes Arkády, Kiríll, and Zakháry, all survived. However, the old patriarch perished of heart failure on the return."

He crossed himself before continuing.

"Dear lady"—he went over to Countess Tirÿna and kissed her hand—"I regret to inform you that your esteemed husband, Dónan Count Kosnick, died of his injuries on the second day after the battle, the nineteenth day of June, the stump of his arm having festered, with the poison going into his body. There was nothing the few remaining doctors could do for him."

Tirÿna's face was a study in grief.

"What about my younger sons?" she managed to gasp out.

"I'm truly sorry to say that I don't know what became of

them," Maurin replied. "They were not recorded on the official register of the dead officers, but many bodies were burned beyond recognition. They could have survived and been captured by partisans, and if so, you will undoubtedly receive a demand for ransom. But I did not see them among the survivors, and I cannot offer you much hope, Lady. My heart and that of my wife go out to you."

"My Bödö, what became of him?" asked Pímay Lady Béçin.

"Lord Bödönal was alive at the beginning of the third day at Killingford," Maurin said, "but I never saw him thereafter. Again, I'm sorry I have no more information.

"Please!" He held up his hands. "I'll be happy to talk to you individually afterwards. First let me finish what remains to be said about our expedition.

"We returned to Saint Paulinos's," Maurin continued, "but it had been gutted, and our supplies taken or lost. We had about five thousand men left, many of them burned or injured. We began the long trek home, fighting off partisans and irregulars along the way. Fortunately, we still had our horses, and we did meet with some additional supply trains and reinforcements coming up from the south, which helped considerably.

"Still, it was a long, hot, slow, and arduous journey back to the relative safety of Borgösha. The Skopélosz Pass was so crowded with troops and messengers that we had to wait for some days before we could cross. Then we reached Myláßgorod, and since I had been severely injured, although now partially recovered, I asked to be released from my commission. This I was allowed to do, but they wouldn't even give me a horse or let me transit to Podébrad. So I started home on foot, determined to get here by any means possible."

"What about the Forellës?" one old man shouted.

"Dead, all of them, and good riddance, too," Lord Maurin replied. "I hear tell that there's an old aunt or two around somewhere, but I don't know if that's true or not. I don't think we'll see them again."

Then Maurin's servant Wyvin came forward, kissed his

master's hand, and raised it up into the air.

"My lords and ladies," he exclaimed, "I give you Count Kosnick!"

"No!" Maurin shouted. "No! Please stop, Wyvin. I appreciate the sentiments, but we simply do not know if Count Dónan's sons are really dead. I will allow three months from this day for them to return home or for a notice of ransom to arrive here, and if nothing comes, then we can take the appropriate steps. Milady Countess, please accept my apologies."

With great dignity the Countess Tirÿna rose to her feet, and came quietly over to Maurin, hugging him very tightly. They could see her shoulders shaking with sobs. Then she turned a tear-stained face to the multitude.

"I'm sorry, dear Maurin," she managed to choke out, "but Wyvin's right. There's so much to do now, and we cannot allow a lapse in government at this crucial time. *Someone* must take charge. If you will not be named Count, then you must at least be Regent, and I do so nominate you, pending confirmation by the king."

Count Maurinos peered around at the semicircle of faces waiting for him to do something, and then looked for the dear image of his wife. When she came over, he pulled her close under his shoulder.

"God will testify that I did not seek this honor," he stated, "but I also do not have the right to reject the responsibility."

There were ragged cheers from the crowd.

Then he turned to Countess Tirÿna, and kissed her gently on the forehead.

"Cousine," he said, "you will never want for anything as long as I live. Your daughters will have dowries, and all of you will always have a place in my heart and in my home. I do so swear, upon my honor as a Markstadt. So help me, God.

"Now, my dear friends and cousins," he continued, "we have much work to do. Please sit with me, and I will tell you what I can of your menfolk. I am counting upon all of you to help us through this difficult time."

And history has recorded that Maurinos III Count von Kosnick was one of the greatest representatives of his line, a fair and generous ruler whose name has ever been venerated as an exemplar of the best that a man can be.

CHAPTER THIRTY-SEVEN
"SHRIVE ME BEFORE I DIE"

On the Feast of Saint Asaphos, the fourth day after Killingford, the broken remnants of the Kórynthi army finally reached Saint Paulinos's again. But instead of the neatly-tended orchards, vineyards, and gardens that they had found on their previous visit, there was nothing left save burned fields, gutted rooms, and the scattered remnants of their baggage.

Of Prince Norbert, now the Forellëan heir to the throne of Pommerelia, who had been sent back to the abbey with five hundred men on the second day of the battle, in order to provide additional security for the women and the supply trains, they saw no sign. After much searching, one of the scouts discovered a burial pit a half mile away, and in it they found the rotting bodies of several hundred Kórynthi soldiers. Norbert's *corpus* was not among them. It took some uncomfortable period of time to determine this with any certainty.

With the death of the patriarch several days before, and the loss of half of the Holy Synod at Killingford, the Archpriest Athanasios was now the senior surviving member of the church on the expedition. The events of the previous week had thoroughly shaken the cleric. Never had he seen such carnage or so many terrible injuries, and never had he so doubted the mercy of his God. But he had spent himself in his work, trying to help as much as possible the handful of physicians who were still functional, and he had been present to comfort Patriarch Avraäm when he had finally succumbed to his last attack of the heart.

The old churchman had removed his inscribed signet ring, and had handed it to Athanasios.

"My brother in Christ," he had said, "put this emblem on your finger to take to Metropolitan Timotheos. He's a good man and a strong man, and he should lead the church after me, if those old fools have any sense at all. Tell him also that I commend you to him as successor in his see. Give me your blessing, father, and shrive me before I die."

The priest had done both, gladly.

Now Athanasios was being asked to serve the role of church representative on the War Council, until another could be appointed. They had cleared one of the less damaged rooms in the abbey, and erected makeshift benches there.

"My friends and brothers," Prince Arkády said, "I don't have to tell you what a parlous state we're in. We have roughly five thousand men left; a third of these are injured, some quite seriously. Supplies are low, and we've found nothing here to eat. Prince Norbert and his stepmother, sister, and sister-in-law are all missing and presumed dead or captured. The king's tent is burned, and the transit mirror destroyed. We carry with us the remains of my brother, Prince Nikolaí, as well as Prince Ezzö, King Humfried, Patriarch Avraäm, Prince Pankratz, Lord Tivadar the Hankyárar, Lord Navkráty, and many others—may they rest in peace!—pickled in brine and preserved in stasis."

He paused, visibly moved.

"However, on the good side, we are apparently *not* being pursued by the Pommerelians, except for raids by the irregulars, and so we must assume that they have suffered losses comparable to our own. Also, many of our horses were saved, so we don't lack for transportation. I have ordered our surviving scouts and other volunteers to ride constant patrols, particularly to the south, to try and locate any word of *Junior* or the other survivors. Already, we've stumbled across twenty men hiding in ravines near Killingford, and have brought them back safely.

"I propose that we wait here two more days," he said, "and then begin the long trek home. Any comments or questions?"

"What about the king?" Prince Kiríll asked. "Shouldn't we ask his opinion?"

Arkády sighed. "King Kipriyán was severely shocked during the final attack at Killingford, and has not been himself since then. He blames the Dark-Haired Man for what has happened, and believes that we should press our advantage now that we've beaten the Pommerelians. Does anyone support this position?"

He pointedly gazed around the room at the surviving council members. Kiríll looked down uncomfortably at the floor.

"Barring any disagreement, we will proceed as outlined," Arkády said. "This council is adjourned."

As they drifted away to their posts, Father Athanasios inadvertently overheard Prince Kiríll talking with his brother, Prince Zakháry.

"I hear that Papá is still being tended by that charlatan, Melanthrix," said Zakháry. "Damned insolent bastard. *That's* the only thing wrong with the king."

"Not so loud!" Kiríll said, "Arkády might hear you. He's the one who's letting that quack treat father with his potions. I hear Melanthrix was responsible for the failed working."

"What!" Zakháry said. "I thought Humfried suggested that."

"Oh, he did!" his brother said. "But it was Melanthrix who showed him how to do it, and it was Melanthrix who was watching constantly from the battlements. *I* say that he fudged it, brother, he soured the magic, and then he blamed poor Humfried when it all went wrong."

"Well, if *that's* true, then I wonder what else he's done," Zakháry said. "I don't like the way he hangs around Arkády's family, either. He's got Kásha's wife jumping every time little Ari has one of his attacks. You know, he didn't start having these 'fits' until Melanthrix showed up."

"Yes, and that's not all," Kiríll said. "There was also the time...."

But they had drifted too far out of Afanásy's range for him to hear the rest, and he couldn't follow them without being too obvious. Instead, he sought out Prince Arkády.

"Highness," he said.

"Yes, Father Athanasios," the prince said. "I'm rather busy right now, so unless it's important...."

"I thought you'd like to know about something I just heard," the priest said, and proceeded to tell Arkády about his younger brothers' conversation.

"Hmm," the prince said. "There's nothing I can do about it now, but I'd like you to keep your ears open, father, and report any further discussions of this type. In the meantime, there's something you can help me with. Tonight I want to try contacting my sister Arrhiána in Paltyrrha, and we'll need a number of Psairothi adepts in the link to get enough power to reach her at that distance. I'm thinking of using you, my brothers, several of the doctors, and anyone else you can suggest as part of the chain. Meet me here at sundown."

Later that day, as darkness fell over Saint Paulinos's, nine mages met in the same room that they had been using for the council meetings. They sat together in a circle. After they had centered themselves, they grasped the hands on either side of them, making certain that their rings were touching, and then waited for Prince Arkády's guidance.

Using their combined energies, the prince mentally reached out towards the east, trying desperately to touch Arrhiána's mind through the leys.

CHAPTER THIRTY-EIGHT
"ANYTHING COULD
HAVE HAPPENED"

Back in Paltyrrha, the princess was scrolling through a collection of verse in the old tongue by the ancient poetess Åyyá, when the page she was reading blurred, and she had a glimpse of a darkened ruin and nine men in a circle. She felt a nagging itch in the back of her consciousness, and tried to focus on the source, but without success.

Again, the group from Saint Paulinos's tried to transmit a message, and again they failed to make contact. Finally, they gave up.

"We'll try once more tomorrow," the prince said, as they went their separate ways.

But Princess Arrhiána sought out Princess Dúra.

"I think Arkády just tried to reach me," she said, "but we couldn't link up."

"Are you sure it was him?" Dúra asked.

"Not positively," Arrhiána said, "but the direction was right, and I don't know who else it could be. You heard that the *viridaurum* in father's tent has been inoperative for four days. I'm very worried about the situation there. The last we heard, they were anticipating a big battle somewhere north of Balíxira. Then nothing. Of course, anything could have happened to the transit point; they're very difficult to keep operational when being moved around constantly. If this *was* Arkády, then he'll try again tomorrow night, and we need to be ready for him. Can you gather together some of the ladies?"

"Sachette, maybe?" Dúra asked. "And I hear Brisquayne just came back: she'd be another possibility. Teréza and Polyxena could also be included."

"Brisquayne's back already?" Arrhiána asked.

"Oh, yes," Dúra said. "Her new great-grandson was finally born, perfectly healthy, and she decided to return early. I'm not sure why. I saw her just briefly this afternoon before she transited to Kórynthály."

"Then by all means invite her," Arrhiána said, "and the others as well. I'll see who else I can find. I do hope Papá and my brothers are all right."

"Oh, Rhie, so do I," Dúra said.

CHAPTER THIRTY-NINE
"HAVE YOU CONFIRMED THIS?"

The next day was the Feast of Saint Akakios the Martyr. At midday the scout Çévik asked to see Prince Arkády privately, and gave him the news that he had been expecting to hear.

"Have you confirmed this?" he asked.

"Yes, sir," the chief scout said. "I saw it posted myself in Balíxira."

"You've done well," the prince said. "Continue the patrols today, but have everyone here by tomorrow morning for further instructions."

"Aye, Highness," Çévik said.

He saluted briskly before leaving.

The prince called the council together again that afternoon, and wasted no time in apprising them of the new situation.

"Our scouts have obtained some information that you need to hear," he said. "King Barnim was killed at the river, or died shortly thereafter"—"Praise God!" Prince Kiríll interjected—"and has been succeeded by his eldest son, Prince Walther. They're calling Killingford a victory, saying that the invaders were defeated, but the truth, at least according to what Çévik believes, is that their losses were at least as severe as our own.

"However, before you rejoice too much, we've learned that Prince Norbert was captured together with his women, and that the prince will be tried for treason at Balíxira several days hence. I don't have to tell you what the outcome of that trial will be. We don't have the men to take Balíxira, even if the Pommerelian army had collapsed completely, which I can't believe it has. We're surrounded by hostile forces, we have minimal provisions and many wounded, and in my estimation, we need to get home. With the king incapacitated, I need to hear your opinions before making a decision."

Prince Zakháry raised his hand.

"I've had a chance to examine in more detail the readiness of our forces," he said, "and we're just not capable of mounting much of a fight. We lost most of our gear at Killingford, along with our supplies and the cream of our soldiery. If we start home now, we should be able to locate foodstuffs along the way, either from our own wagons or from whatever the local farmers have left. The partisans are no match for us. If we wait, Pommerelia will be forced to come after us, and I don't think either side wants that, just now. So I vote for a strategic withdrawal."

He chuckled, but there was no humor in the laugh.

"I agree," said Prince Kiríll. "We'll be lucky to get our injured men back safe."

There was no dissension.

"I also concur," Arkády said. "Very well, on the morrow we'll break camp. I want our engines and any surviving buildings here burnt to the ground, together with any non-essential supplies. Begin gathering them at once. Are there any other matters to discuss?"

Zakháry spoke up.

"I charge Doctor Melanthrix with treason," he said, "for disrupting the working at Killingford."

"I join with my brother," said Kiríll.

Arkády sighed, and paused a moment before responding.

"I will take your charge under advisement," he said, "until we reach Paltyrrha. Now is not the time for recriminations. We need to find the best and quickest way home. That means that *all* of us must work together towards a common end. We have already sacrificed five-sixths of our force; we can't afford to lose any others. The king should hear this accusation; if he is unable to, I will act on it at Tighrishály."

The prince looked around the makeshift table, focusing particularly on his two brothers.

"I must ask you not to comment on this further," he said. "In the meantime, I have an important task for each of you. We will try to reach our sister again this evening, but I suspect that the distance is just too great with the mountains intervening. It's imperative that we make contact with home as quickly as possible, both to apprise them of our situation and to indicate what we will need for our men upon returning.

"Therefore, I am sending Prince Kiríll, Prince Zakháry, and Father Athanasios on a special mission. Tomorrow morning, at the same time we break camp, you will ride ahead on the fastest mounts we have, changing them at Karkára, and again whenever you meet with any of our men. Kiríll, you'll take command at Karkára. Zakháry, you'll assume command at Borgösha. Your tasks will be to secure our rear guard, get us supplies as quickly as possible, and clear the Skopélosz Pass so we can move our wounded through to the motherland.

"Father Athanasios, I want you to ride all the way through to Myláßgorod, and discretely inform Count Zygmunt of our situation. You will order him to secure his side of the Skopélosz, and to stop the flow of troops and wagons from the east. Then you will transit to Paltyrrha, and quietly and confidentially tell my sister and the *Locum Tenens* of the Holy Church what has happened here. Finally, after completing these tasks, you are further ordered to find and secure the Forellëan heir, the Princess Arizélla, and to bring her at once to Paltyrrha, with or without her cooperation.

"I will provide all three of you with the appropriate passes, and a special message for you, father, to take to my sister. You may commandeer whatever escort you need, but given the fact that there are irregular Pommerelian forces roaming everywhere, you might do better to emphasize speed over security.

"You will operate in total secrecy, and carry out my orders to the letter. Anyone opposing you will be considered traitors to the Kórynthi crown. Understood?"

"Yes, Highness," they said.

"Very well," Arkády said. "You're all dismissed, except for Athanasios."

He turned to the priest.

"Father," he said, "I need you to take down a letter to Princess Arrhiána, and to prepare several passes."

CHAPTER FORTY
"SOMEPLACE MORE PRIVATE"

Later that evening, the nine adepts at St. Paulinos tried again to reach Paltyrrha, but were ultimately frustrated by the tantalizing sense that with just a little more concentration, they might actually have broken through.

Back in the capital, however, Princess Arrhiána and her four ladies were able to confirm the contact, if not the message.

"Well, we *do* know they're alive," the princess said, "at least some of them. It was definitely Arkády."

"But what was he trying to say?" Dúra asked.

"I just don't know," Arrhiána said. "I sensed an undercurrent of trouble, so I don't think the news is good, whatever it is. All we can do is pray, and try again tomorrow evening."

As the ladies prepared to depart, Dowager Queen Brisquayne stopped Arrhiána.

"I wonder if I might speak with you," she said.

"Of course, Granny," Arrhiána said. "I always have time for you. How was your trip to Neustria?"

"That's what I wanted to discuss," the older woman said. "I wonder if you have someplace more private where we could talk? Maybe even protected?"

Arrhiána glanced sharply at Brisquayne. This was most unusual. She had never known the woman to be more than a gossipy, ebullient busybody.

"Come to my chambers," she said, leading the way. "How's the baby?"

"My great-grandson is fine, and so are my children and grandchildren," Granny said, while walking with the princess. "It's nothing about them, although I guess maybe it is, in a way. I don't know, anymore. I shouldn't say anything else until we're protected."

In Arrhiána's quarters was a small windowless room, a study almost, that she had carefully sealed against all psychic intruders, including some that weren't Psairothi. It required the princess's deliberate physical touch even to allow the passage of an individual other than herself into the space.

"Will this do?" she asked.

Brisquayne looked around the room, and extended her senses in all directions.

"Most impressive," the queen said.

Arrhiána smiled. "You're not quite the person you sometimes appear to be, are you, Granny?" she said.

"Well," Brisquayne said, "no one pays any attention to an old fool."

She cleared her throat, clearly uncomfortable about continuing with this subject.

"Arrhiána," she said, "something happened while I was in Lavallière that caused me great concern. You've heard my stories about your great-aunt, the Princess Mösza, who was a contemporary of mine lo these many years ago. We discussed her during your recent visit to Kórynthály. She disappeared during the last war under somewhat strained circumstances, and I had thought her long dead. Well, I was wrong."

"What?" the princess said. "Wouldn't she be too old?"

"Not really," the dowager queen said. "She was about my age, which would put her in her mid-sixties now. She turned up under a new guise and name, suddenly acting as midwife for the birth of Prince Chilpéric, my great-grandson, and she attacked my granddaughter, Princess Brislaine, while she was giving birth. If I hadn't been there, if I hadn't fought Mösza for control of my granddaughter's body, Laine could have died, and the baby with her."

"Why would she *do* such a thing?" Arrhiána asked.

"I don't know." Brisquayne sat back with downcast eyes. "It's been forty years at least since I last saw Mösza. I think I was her only friend when she was still living in Kórynthia. She was a shy girl, neglected as a child and bedeviled by her own fancies. I think her mother, Dowager Hereditary Princess Zubayda, always associated the girl with the passing of Hereditary Prince Karlomán, Zubayda's husband and Mösza's father, who died young about the time she was born.

"Then, too, Mösza was the last child in a big family—her brother, King Makáry, was twenty years her senior—and there just never seemed to be enough love to go around for someone who really needed special attention. She was bright, almost too bright for her own good, and had no social sense at all. Her plain looks didn't help matters any. Although most members of her family were chasing after the bunnies in the fields or anything else that moved by the time they were fifteen, Mösza was the exception to the rule. She never showed much interest in boys, or really in anything except her own avocations.

"I felt sorry for Mösza, and so I tried spending some extra time with her. I knew very well what it was like to be a social outcast, since I had lived much of my early life in a similar situation. I guess I just coped better. She was very well read—books were her first love—so we could always talk about literature, a favorite avocation of mine as well.

"She changed quite a bit during those last few months at court. Then, like now, we were fighting a major war against Pommerelia, and the atmosphere at home was very tense. When the word came of King Makáry's death, and the passing of his two elder sons, she just seemed to go to pieces before us. I only saw her once after that, and then she was gone, hustled off to God knows where by Zubayda and Víktor."

"What possible motive could she have had for this attack?" the princess asked.

"I'm not sure that there is any motive we would understand," Brisquayne said. "When I touched her psychically, I sensed a reservoir of malice there against all members of the House of Tighris; of course, both of my daughters were children of King Makáry. I also had the distinct impression that she was sending me a message, to keep my mouth shut about olden times at court, or risk the consequences. Which brings me to a very interesting question: how did she hear? If this attack *was* deliberate, how could she have known what I said to a handful of people in my own home? It wasn't my servants. I've already eliminated that possibility. One of us had to have talked about the visit to a third party."

"It wasn't Arkády or me, that I can vouch for," Arrhiána said. "That leaves Sachette and Rÿna. I'll ask Chette, but I strongly doubt it was her. She has more sense than to talk about such things, and until she left the cloister recently, had had no visitors except us. Well, let's start with my sister, and then we can question Rÿna very carefully later on. Little girls are easily manipulated by outsiders.

"Can you think of anything else that might have happened when Mösza was at court that could have prompted this?"

"Oh, Rhie," Brisquayne said, "I've just been turning this over and over in my mind since I saw 'Mirza,' as she was calling herself in Neustria. She broke off her attack when I flashed her a picture of her brother and his sons riding out of Paltyrrha on that fateful day forty-odd years ago. Something about it upset her terribly. I remember overhearing a couple of the women at court talking together not long before Mösza disappeared. I didn't hear the whole conversation, and no names were mentioned, so I didn't pay much attention, and never heard anything else along these lines again. It went something like this:

"'You're *joking*!'

"'Well, that's what one of the maids said,' said the second voice, giggling.

"'So what are they going to *do* about it?' the first voice asked.

"'I *don't* know,' said the second, 'but I heard her mother was absolutely livid. She was storming around her rooms shouting, "Unnatural bitch," "Salomé," "Beast," and other such things, and slapping the girl around this way and that, and threatening to denounce her to the church.'

"'Oh, God, I wish I could have been there!' the first woman said.

"'And then she brought her brother in, and he said he was going to ex-, uh, *ex-com-mun-i-cate* her, and she said—get this—*that she didn't care*, that they were all a bunch of *hypo-cricks*, whatever that is.'

"The second person snickered again.

"'This is priceless. Wait until Buïela hears this!' number one said."

"Buïela was a well-known gossip-mongerer at court then," the old queen said.

"'Well, I repeat, *whatever* are they going to do?' the first woman said.

"'What *can* they do?' said the second. 'Why, I wouldn't be surprised if they didn't ship her off somewhere until the you-know-what happens.'

"'You mean she's actually....' The first lady started laughing.

"'That's what I hear,' replied the second, still giggling. 'Uh oh, let's get out of here: someone's coming,' she added in a lower tone of voice."

Brisquayne sighed.

"Ladies came and went at court fairly regularly in those days," she said, "particularly during the war. Although I hadn't seen these two, I knew exactly who they were. As I said, I never thought too much about their conversation at the time—so many things were going on then—but in thinking back about it now, I don't believe I ever saw them at court again. And I know very well that Buïela never heard the tale, because giving her something was like telling it to the whole wide world.

"So, I now think that these two ladies knew something they shouldn't have known, some secret that was quietly and efficiently covered up. Remember, it was right after this time that the king was killed and Zubayda and Víktor became regents for young King Kipriyán, giving them effective control of the state until Kipriyán came of age."

"*That's* quite a story," Arrhiána said. "Do you think Mösza had a *liaison* with someone at court?"

"Well, if this *was* her they were talking about," the queen said, "that would be *my* conclusion. It fits the facts. But if so, then she must have been seduced. There's no possible way that the girl *I* knew would have initiated an intimate contact with *anyone*: she was just too frightened and too inexperienced, even though she was almost twenty-five years old then. She had never made the leap into adulthood."

"And if her mother had then berated her for her weakness...," Arrhiána said.

"...She would have reacted very badly, I think," Brisquayne said. "She had a fragile personality. She might well have become embittered and vengeful."

"Is there any way to confirm this, or to find out more?" Arrhiána asked.

"I've done a great deal of thinking, Rhie," the queen said, "about who might still remember those days, but that was a long time ago, and most everyone who was present at court then is long dead."

"What about those two you overheard?" Arrhiána said.

"I'm not even sure if I can remember their names. At any rate," the queen said, "I'm more concerned about the present. We need to know how Mösza found out about our conversation. When she was banished from Kórynthia for life, as I assume she was, she would have had something implanted into her psyche. If they followed their usual practice, they would have fixed her with a telltale that would have prevented her from ever returning to our soil. It's absolutely diabolical, causing dizziness, nausea, and convulsions in the recipient, and it can't be removed, ever. We don't do things like that very much today, but back then, it did happen, albeit infrequently."

"I've only heard of such things indirectly," Arrhiána said, "but you're absolutely right, of course. If she can't even step on Kórynthi soil, then *how* did she know?"

Arrhiána kissed and hugged her step-grandmother.

"Never fear, Granny," she said, "we'll find out, and we'll make certain that all of your family is safe. Now, let's get back to the others, before someone wonders where we've gone."

CHAPTER FORTY-ONE
"DON'T GET
YOURSELVES KILLED"

The following day was Sunday, the Feast of Saint Mölray, and Hereditary Prince Arkády decreed that the surviving members of the expedition would celebrate a mass of remembrance before breaking camp. The Archpriest Athanasios, as the senior church member present, presided over the services.

"Almighty God," he intoned over the bowed heads of the soldiers and their officers, "we call upon You to remember the souls of those who have fought the good fight and who have departed this earth, and to bless your servants Avraäm, Nikolaí, Humfried, Pankratz, Ezzö, and all the others who died at Killingford, that they may rejoice in life eternal, and sing Your praises forever and ever. Amen."

"Amen," said the multitude.

"And we ask You, oh Lord," he said, "to show us the way home, to light a path for us, to let us bring these wounded men and boys back to full health and happiness. Have mercy, oh Lord, on these Your humble servants, and forgive us our sins. Amen."

"Amen," came the refrain.

"May Almighty God bless, preserve, and restore you to ever-lasting peace," he said, giving them his benediction.

"God save Prince Arkády!" he suddenly added.

"*God save Prince Arkády!*" came the thunderous response.

Then they began to break this camp of sorrows. The scout

Çévik organized a party to torch the pile of engines and excess baggage they had accumulated the previous evening. Anything that might slow them down, including very large weaponry, was sacrificed. Another group set fire to the empty monastery, going from room to room with their torches, and salvaging only a barrel of wine that had somehow been missed by the earlier scavengers.

At last the princes mounted the horses. Prince Arkády clasped hands with his two brothers, and wished them well.

"Don't get yourselves killed," he said.

"Not a chance," Kiríll said, a crooked grin appearing on his face. "Zack and I will just have to make sure that Father Athanasios keeps up."

He adjusted his greatbow on his shoulder, flexing his injured arm, which was almost back to normal strength.

"And you, Prince Arkády," Athanasios said, "you also be watchful. Take good care of these men."

"I shall, father," the prince said.

And then they were off!

Behind them a great column of smoke reached into the sky, marking the end of their hopes in Pommerelia. Their kinsmen here would have to find their own saviors. The Tighrishi could no longer offer a way out.

The three men rode east and then slightly southeast, following the main road toward Karkára, which was still in Kórynthi hands. They encountered the first wagon train a little after midday, and directed it onward to service the main army. They stumbled across the remains of a second train later in the afternoon, scaring off the vultures tearing at the bones of its dead guards. There was no sign of the partisans who had done this outrage.

"Thorough, aren't they?" Zakháry said.

"Yes, brother, and they will happily do the same to us if they catch us loitering here," Kiríll said.

Athanasios insisted on saying a prayer of remembrance over the remains, despite the protests of the two princes. Then they spurred their horses forward, the priest trailing in their wake.

About an hour before sunset they encountered a party of ten Pommerelians, who loosed several arrows at them, and then tried to ride them down. When it became obvious to the trio that their tired mounts simply could not carry them out of danger, Prince Zakháry ordered a halt after rounding a bend in the road, and hid them in the brush on either side. He and his brother quickly strung their bows, and waited.

As the raiding party came around the corner, the two princes brought down four of the Pommerelians immediately, including their leader, and nailed a fifth as he turned to flee. The other five retreated, and began lobbing bolts back in the other direction. Neither side was able to move until sunset, when Zakháry carefully maneuvered them down the road on foot, leading the horses, fresh now from their enforced rest.

Then they remounted, and took off again. This time they were not followed.

They reached the Kórynthi camp in Lüstern Field at the base of the Karkára Cut not long after sunrise the next day. There Prince Kiríll presented his credentials, and was escorted to the castle he had taken just the month before.

Prince Zakháry and Father Athanasios were outfitted with new steeds, and given a chance for a good meal and brief rest. The two brothers embraced, and bid each other *bonne chance*. Zakháry and Athanasios then turned their steeds down the long, tired, crowded road to Borgösha.

EPILOGUE
"SOMETHING HAS AMUSED YOUR MAJESTY?"

Anno Domini 1241
Anno Juliani 881

When Count Maurin had finally finished the main part of his tale, the hour was late, and Queen Grigorÿna was tempted to break for the evening. But she sensed that the nobleman still had ought to say, and knew that if she delayed the telling till another day, he might not speak the same again. And so she let him continue.

"Slowly and carefully," he said, "Hereditary Prince Arkády pulled the remnants of our tattered army back over the mountains into Kórynthia, taking care, however, to preserve such lands in Pommerelia as were needed for the protection of our forces—and for the future integrity of the realm.

"These he set off with a series of forts anchored around the main towns flanking the mountain range on the west, making certain that they had sufficient of our forces to defend themselves from any likely attack in the near future.

"I was given command of some of the mostly-destroyed remnants of the army units that had been enmeshed in the center of the fight at Killingford, including a great many soldiers who'd been wounded, either in body or in spirit; and was ordered to bring them safely back to the motherland.

"This I did.

"Then I received my discharge, and slowly walked the entire distance back to Kosnickland. There were simply no horses or other beasts to spare, and the few transit portals were continually occupied with official business.

"I was desperate to see my people again—and also felt compelled to relay to them whatever news I had (most of it not good) of their loved ones.

"And this was the end of my involvement with the Great War. I transited once or twice to Paltyrrha before the end of the year, but of the huge events that reshaped the realm that fall, I have no direct knowledge. I did not participate in them or witness what took place."

Then he lapsed into solitude, and she knew that he'd finally finished.

She asked him a series of questions about the great working that had destroyed the major parts of both combatants' armies, but although he'd undergone basic Psairothi training, he understood almost nothing of what had occurred.

"What was attempted by Melanthrix and the others was so far above the level of my skill that I might as well have been a five-year-old just starting to draw my letters. I *saw* what happened, to be sure, but it was so much fire and brimstone to me. I do know that I was lucky to escape alive from that conflagration: most of the men on the field did not share my fortune, I'm sorry to say."

She pressed him further for details, and then for a list of survivors of the battle who might yet live, and he tried to help her as best as could—but at last she realized that she had reached a point where nothing would be gained by continuing. She offered him a room for the night, but he declined.

"I must return home; my dear wife expects me," was all that he could say.

She thanked him for his time, and asked him if there was something she could do to benefit his people; and when he mentioned a canal that had long been planned, and even started—but had been deferred for lack of funds—she gladly promised that the throne would provide the sum necessary to complete the project.

And then he left.

* * * * * * *

In the weeks and days that followed, she located some of the survivors who'd been mentioned by the Count, but none them could add anything relevant to her history. Once again she chafed at her restrictions: there *was* one who could have helped her, perhaps greatly, but the Queen feared even attempting to make contact with *that* individual. Only the strongest would or could dare such a venture, and she required some further protections.

In the meantime, she now needed to locate some of those courtiers who'd been present at Paltyrrha when the Hereditary Prince and his father and family had at last returned home, thereby setting in motion the end game of the war—well, the end, at least, of that *particular* game and that particular war.

For 'twas a known truth—and one well appreciated by her— that the universe was filled with malicious spirits who were always playing games of chance or intrigue with their human inferiors; and the best that the player sitting on the hard obsidian throne could ever hope for was a stalement—and never a victory.

But this was today, and not tomorrow, and she would take such troubles as might appear on the horizon when they poked their ugly heads above the rim of the world.

In the meantime, what to do about the puzzlement of her marriage? That was all that her counselors regarded as worth any consideration. None of them, after all, were students of history.

She laughed out loud at the idea.

"Something has amused Your Majesty?" Svyet asked.

Grigorÿna giggled like a little girl.

"Indeed," she said.

AFTERWORD
"HISTORY TELLS US OTHERWISE"

When I wrote *The Dark-Haired Man*, of which this novel was once the middle section, I constructed the book to revolve around the great battle of Killingford.

Many writers of medieval fantasy either glorify battle or sanitize it—or imply that every such conflict had a quick and rather clean-cut conclusion.

History tells us otherwise.

Indeed, there *were* battles—and wars—that ended swiftly, when one side overwhelmed the other. But there were also conflicts between and among states and their allies that continued for decades, devasting the countrysides of the nations in which they were fought, and leaving no real victors to stagger away from the battlefields.

The losers were always the commonfolk.

I wanted to depict a disagreement between states based on religious and cultural differences, the real motivating factors behind so many disputes, both personal and societal. I wanted to show a war that had no clear winners or losers, but would obviously be refought again in the future of this world, perhaps to the same conclusion.

I hope I've succeeded.

The Old King has been driven near to madness by...something or someone hovering in the background. We discover a bit more about this individual in the third novel in the sequence, *'Ware the Dark-Haired Man*. But as to why some folks willingly pursue the dark side of existence, and others follow the light, there are no good answers—either in Nova Europa or on Earth. It happens, although most of us meander somewhere in the middle of the woad.

Prince Arkády is my exemplar of the noble individual who consistently tries to do the right thing—by his father, by his state, by his church, by his family—some of these being at various times one and the same entities. But this is not always possible in a real or even in a make-believe world, because no one's vision is clear enough to determine the right path in every instance. The best that one can sometimes do is try—and then hope for the best.

As for the Prince's father, the King, he too becomes a prisoner of his past and present, of sins contemplated and committed—by him and by others in his family. These books are, essentially, moral tales about family life and family tensions, when that family absolutely controls the destiny of the state. The political mirror in which their actions are reflected magnifies both their errors and their sometime righteousness.

As for the Princess (later Queen) Grigorÿna, we know from other passages in these fables that her character was essentially established at a young age through the influence of potent mages and manipulators. To what extent she has been affected in later life by these early experiences, we have no idea. She was a strange little girl, and she has become, in some sense, a strange middle-aged woman. But that fact is not especially strange in the overall context of her family history.

So I hope you enjoy my little excursions into worldplay as much as I did when I created Nova Europa. This three-novel sequence, originally consisting of one very large fantasy, reflects the best writing experience that I've ever had. The book just "flowed"—it poured out of me in one large gush of creativity—and I remain today in awe of what happened during those months, while knowing full well that the same event is unlikely to repeat itself, for many different reasons (including the fact that I'm a different person than I was back then).

If you like my work, you can find me through my website...

www.robertreginald.com

—Robert Reginald
San Bernardino, California
28 November 2012

ABOUT THE AUTHOR

ROBERT REGINALD was born in Japan, and lived in Turkey as a youth, plus a half dozen different U.S. states. He starting writing as a child, and penned his first book during his senior year at Gonzaga University. He settled in Southern California in 1969, where he served as an academic librarian for forty years. He currently edits the Borgo Press imprint for Wildside Press, having turned in some 1,200 volumes in seven years, and has also penned more than 137 books and 13,000 short pieces.

His fiction titles include: twelve Nova Europa historical fantasies in four trilogies (2004-13): *Melanthrix the Mage*, *Killingford*, *'Ware the Dark-Haired Man*, *The Righteous Regicide*, *The Virgin Queens*, *The Prince of Exiles*, *Brother Theo's God*, *Questions and Questings*, *Whither Goest Thou?*, *The Cracks in the Æther*, *The Pachyderms' Lament*, and *The Fourth Elephant's Egg*; The War of Two Worlds science fiction trilogy: *Invasion!*, *Operation: Crimson Storm*, and *The Martians Strike Back!* (2007/2011); a science fiction novel in The Human-Knacker War series: *Knack' Attack* (2010); a future dystopia, *Academentia* (2011); two Phantom Detective period mysteries: *The Phantom's Phantom* (2007) and *The Nasty Gnomes* (2008); a comic mystery, *The Paperback Show Murders* (2011); and three short story collections: *Katydid & Other Critters: Tales of Fantasy and Mystery* (2001), *The Elder of Days: Tales of the Elders* (2010), *The Judgment of the Gods and Other Verdicts of History* (2011).

He's also edited several anthologies: *Choice Words: The*

Borgo Press Book of Writers Writing on Writing (2010), *Yondering: The First Borgo Press Book of Science Fcition Stories* (2011), *To the Stars—and Beyond: The Second Borgo Press Book of Science Fcition Stories* (2011), *Once Upon a Future: The Third Borgo Press Book of Science Fcition Stories* (2011), *Whodunit?: The First Borgo Press Book of Crime and Mystery Stories* (2011); *More Whodunits: The Second Borgo Press Book of Crime and Mystery Stories* (2011), *The Christmas Megapack: Yuletide Stories* (2012), and *The Second Christmas Megapack: Yuletide Stories* (2012).

You can find him at:

www.robertreginald.com

www.ingramcontent.com/pod-product-compliance
Lightning Source LLC
Chambersburg PA
CBHW031423250626
47155CB00004B/1606